THE
GENTLEMAN OUTLAW AND ME—ELI

OTHER BOOKS BY
MARY DOWNING HAHN

Look for Me by Moonlight

Time for Andrew

The Wind Blows Backward

Stepping on the Cracks

The Spanish Kidnapping Disaster

The Dead Man in Indian Creek

The Doll in the Garden

December Stillness

Following the Mystery Man

Tallahassee Higgins

Wait Till Helen Comes

Daphne's Book

The Time of the Witch

THE
GENTLEMAN OUTLAW AND ME—ELI

A STORY OF THE OLD WEST

BY MARY DOWNING HAHN

CLARION BOOKS
NEW YORK

Clarion Books
a Houghton Mifflin Company imprint
215 Park Avenue South, New York, NY 10003
Text copyright © 1996 by Mary Downing Hahn

Type is 12/15-point New Baskerville.

For information about this and other Houghton Mifflin trade and
reference books and multimedia products, visit The Bookstore
at Houghton Mifflin on the World Wide Web at
(http://www.hmco.com/trade/).

Printed in the USA.

Library of Congress Cataloging-in-Publication Data
Hahn, Mary Downing.
The Gentleman Outlaw and me—Eli: a story of the Old West /
by Mary Downing Hahn.
p.   cm.
Summary: In 1887 twelve-year-old Eliza, disguised as a boy and traveling
toward Colorado in search of her missing father, falls in with
a Gentleman Outlaw and joins him in his illegal schemes.
ISBN 0-395-73083-X
[1. Frontier and pioneer life—West (U.S.)—Fiction.
2. West (U.S.)—Fiction. 3. Robbers and outlaws—Fiction.]   I. Title.
PZ7.H1256Ge   1996
[Fic]—dc20   95-18802
CIP
AC

BP 10 9 8 7 6 5 4 3 2 1

For Eric and Meredith Downing
who love adventures
and
in memory of Harry Sheffield Sherwood
1879–1949
who spun a few western yarns himself

->-•-<-

THE
GENTLEMAN OUTLAW AND ME—ELI

I GOT THE IDEA TO RUN AWAY THE NIGHT Uncle Homer beat me for spilling a glass of milk. I hadn't done it on purpose, and I was genuinely sorry because I was hungry and knew full well I wouldn't get a second glass. But he took his belt to me anyway, and no one said a word in my defense.

Fair didn't enter into it. My cousins spilled milk like it was water going over Niagara Falls and never got a whipping, but I wasn't on an equal level with Millicent, William, and Little Homer. I was a charity case, pure and simple.

Of course, there's some history behind all this. About seven years ago, when I was five, my father got fed up with farming and decided to head west. Nothing Mama said could change his mind. No matter how she begged and pleaded, Papa was bound and determined to try his luck at prospecting. Others were getting rich. Why not him too?

While Papa sought his fortune in Colorado, Mama

and I stayed in Kansas with her sister's family. Aunt Mabel and Uncle Homer treated us all right at first. Like Mama and me, they expected Papa to get rich. No doubt they imagined he'd reward them for taking good care of his wife and daughter.

Then a terrible thing happened. After we'd been at Aunt Mabel's house for a couple of years, Mama took sick and died which is all I can say without crying because I still have a big empty place in my heart where she used to be.

Not long after that, my life took an even worse turn. Papa's letters stopped coming. My kindly kin told me he didn't want me anymore. Which wasn't any wonder, they said, as I was nothing to brag about.

Without Mama to protect me, I soon found myself living the life of a slave, fetching and carrying and doing all the chores whilst my cousins mocked and teased me. The night I spilled the milk, I decided I'd had more than enough of Uncle Homer's belt and Aunt Mabel's spiteful tongue. The next time my uncle took a notion to whip me, I'd head west. Papa's last letter had come from Tinville, Colorado. I hoped I'd find him there.

→>•<←

I didn't have long to wait. Three days later, my cousin William, the most evil child ever born, climbed on a stool to stick his fingers in the jam jar. When Millicent saw what he was up to, she tried to get some too. Next thing they both fell off the stool and the jam jar hit the floor with a crash loud enough to wake a hibernating bear.

I bet I don't need to tell you what happened next. By the time Aunt Mabel arrived on the scene, Millicent and William were blaming it all on me. Me—who'd been out in the yard pumping a bucket of water and made the mistake of running inside to see what the hullabaloo was about.

"I didn't do it," I said.

But Aunt Mabel wasn't one to take my word over her own precious children's. "Don't you lie to me, Eliza Yates," she said as sharp as you please.

I held up the bucket of water for proof. "I was outside filling this, Aunt Mabel." I turned to Millicent and William, hoping against all hope they'd own up to what they'd done. "Tell the truth for once," I begged.

They looked at me with their big blue eyes. "Eliza done it," William whined.

"She got the water 'cause she was hoping to wash the floor before you saw the jam," Millicent added just as sweet as if she were an angel from heaven instead of a fiend from you-know-where.

"Look at their clothes," I said. "They got jam all over themselves!"

"That's 'cause we were trying to tidy up," Millicent

said in this simpering little voice she uses to hide her true nature.

"Yes, Mama, that's exactly what we were doing," said William, always one to agree with his sister. "We were cleaning up the mess Eliza made."

At that moment, Little Homer came up behind me and pinched my arm most painfully. Of my three cousins, he was the worst for hurting me, mainly because he was one year older than me and the biggest, meanest thirteen-year-old ever to breathe Kansas air.

"I seen it all," Little Homer said. "Eliza done it."

"You don't know anything about it, you big lying jackass!" I hollered, mad to the roots of my hair. "You were behind the barn, smoking one of Uncle Homer's cigars. I saw you!"

That did it. Aunt Mabel hauled off and slapped me once or twice. "I don't know which is worse," she yelled. "Stealing jam or lying about it! It's a blessing your poor mother's dead and gone and can't see how you've turned out. You got your father's wild ways along with his red hair."

Once she started into scolding, Aunt Mabel never stopped till sundown, so I just went on about my business, mopping the kitchen floor and thinking my own thoughts. By the time Uncle Homer stepped through the door and started loosening his belt, I was glad he was about to give me the excuse I needed to run.

After supper I did my chores as usual. For once I hardly minded washing the dishes and scrubbing the pots and mopping and sweeping and doing whatever else Aunt Mabel thought needed doing. I kept thinking it was the last time I'd see those ugly blue-flowered plates, the last time I'd touch that greasy frying pan, the last time I'd clean the big black stove. In fact, it was all I could do not to sing and dance, which surely would have aroused suspicion.

By the time I finished my chores, Millicent was already sound asleep in the bed we shared. Before I blew out the lamp, I took a good, long look at her spiteful little face. Just like one of those pretty china dolls, she was. Not a brain in her head. Just smart enough to open her eyes when she sat up, close them when she lay down, and cry "Mama" if you squeezed her tummy.

Without getting undressed, I slid into bed beside my cousin, being careful not to wake her. In no time, she was up to her usual nocturnal shenanigans, kicking me, hogging the blankets, and pushing me slowly but surely toward the edge of the mattress. Even in her sleep, Millicent was mean.

But it didn't matter anymore. After tonight, I'd never share a bed with her again. Or anybody else. From now on, I swore I'd sleep by myself.

I waited till I heard snores coming from my aunt and uncle's room down the hall. Then I eased out from under the covers. If Millicent woke up, I planned to tell her I was on my way to the outhouse, but she never flicked an eyelash, just spread out and took up more of the bed.

Shoes in hand, I tiptoed to the top of the steps and paused to listen. Uncle Homer was snoring so loud the walls shook, but the only other sound was the crickets chirping outside in the dark.

Avoiding the squeaky spots, I crept downstairs to the kitchen, sneaked my hand into the very bottom of the flour bin, and retrieved two gold coins from Aunt Mabel's secret hiding place. Don't get me wrong. I'm not a thief. That twenty dollars was mine. Every cent of it. Mama left it to me in her will. My aunt claimed she was keeping it safe for me, but I knew I'd never see it again. Not unless I snatched it back.

Next I went to the pantry and helped myself to half a loaf of bread, a jar of jam, which I figured I deserved, some cheese, and a couple of apples.

I bundled the food in one of Aunt Mabel's old napkins, along with my money, a harmonica Papa had left behind, and a rusty jackknife I'd found behind the outhouse.

Before I left, I took one last look at the kitchen where I'd slaved for so long. It gave me great satisfaction to picture Millicent standing at that sink, up to her pretty little elbows in hot soapy water, scrubbing her fingers raw. As for me, I swore I'd never wash another dish, scour a greasy old pot, or mop a floor. No, sir. Those dull days were gone forever. A new life of ease was waiting for me out West and I could hardly wait to begin living it.

T HE MINUTE I STEPPED OFF THE BACK PORCH, Caesar came running to meet me. He wasn't the world's smartest dog, but he knew better than to make a sound. Like me, he'd had more than his share of blows from Uncle Homer's belt.

I dropped to my knees and slung my arms around his shaggy neck. "I'm leaving," I whispered in his ear. "Don't forget me, Caesar."

I swear that dog understood what I was saying. He was a big old mutt, tall enough to look me in the eye when he stood on his hind legs, but right now he was licking my nose like a lost puppy. All the time he was whining like his heart would break.

I started crying then. How was I to go off and leave Caesar with Uncle Homer? Me—the poor dog's only friend? But how could I take him with me? I had no idea how long it would take to get to Tinville. Didn't know where I'd sleep along the way, or what I'd eat.

While I stood there pondering, Caesar whimpered and held out a paw for me to shake, the one trick he knew, the only one I'd had time to teach him.

That did it. I unfastened his chain, and the two of us ran across the yard, scooted over the back fence, and headed down the alley as fast as we could go—which wasn't near as fast as I'd have liked, on account of Caesar stopping every few seconds to sniff something.

At the end of the alley, we came to the railroad tracks. It made no sense to buy a ticket here in Bartlett. Might as well leave a message on Uncle Homer's pillow, telling him exactly how to find me. So, since I was going out West, I headed in that direction, thinking to reach Clark Summit, the next town down the line, sometime before dawn. I'd board the train there.

I hadn't been walking more than an hour when I ran into trouble. Caesar had followed his nose into the woods, hoping to find a rabbit or squirrel to play with, and I was walking on the railroad tracks, balancing like a tightrope artist and daydreaming about my reunion with Papa. All of a sudden, a raggedy man stepped out of the shadows right in front of me. Without even giving me a chance to think about running, he grabbed my wrist and grinned down at me.

"Well, well," he said, "if it ain't Little Red Riding Hood on her way to Granny's house."

He was looking at my bundle of belongings, his eyes gleaming as if he could see everything in there, including my twenty dollars. If ever I'd thought of a wolf in human form, this man was the very image. All shaggy and dirty and smelling worse than a polecat in the rain.

"Let go of me!" I tried pulling away, but he was a lot bigger than I was. Stronger too.

"Ain't nobody told you good little girls should be home in bed this time of night?" he asked in a voice honeyed with false kindness.

I don't know what would have happened if Caesar hadn't come running out of the woods just then. He took one look at that nasty old tramp and lunged at him, proving the meanness Uncle Homer had been trying to teach him hadn't been in vain after all.

Hollering a string of purely bad words, the tramp took off toward Bartlett with Caesar behind him, shredding the man's trousers to pieces with his sharp teeth.

When he was sure the tramp wasn't going to stop running till next week, Caesar wheeled around and trotted back to me. Of course, I praised him and thanked him and kissed him till he was positively dopey with pride. But it took a while for my heart to slow down and my breath to come easy and natural again.

For a moment I considered scampering home like a scared rabbit. What stopped me was the sight of a clothesline in a yard beside the train tracks. At least a dozen pairs of boys' overalls fluttered in the breeze, along with sheets and shirts and petticoats, waving as if they were beckoning to me. What if I snitched a pair of overalls, cut my hair short, and passed myself off as a boy? No tramps would mess with me then. Or even notice me. The world was full of runaway boys heading west to seek their fortunes.

Best of all, Uncle Homer would be searching for a girl once he discovered I was missing. Not that he'd want me back. It was the twenty dollars he'd be after. If I hadn't taken that, he and Aunt Mabel would probably throw a shindig to celebrate my disappearance.

It didn't take more than a minute to sneak across the grass and grab a pair of overalls and a shirt. I picked the oldest and shabbiest ones on the line. Surely nobody'd miss them or want them either.

'Least I hoped not. I didn't like stealing, but how else was I going to get a disguise? I sure couldn't afford to leave one of my gold coins in exchange for some raggedy old clothes.

As soon as I was safe in the woods, I slipped out of my dress and undergarments. Never in my life had I been stark naked outside in the moonlight. Whooping like a banshee, I kicked up my heels and did a little dance to celebrate my freedom. Caesar ran around in circles, wagging his tail and grinning. He was just as happy as I was.

When a cold breeze tiptoed up and down my bare

spine, I gave up dancing and shivered into my new clothes. The overalls were a mite big, but that meant I had growing room, which I sorely needed. Lately I'd been shooting up faster than Jack's beanstalk.

I pulled on my shoes, thanking my stars Aunt Mabel was of a practical mind. When you have a niece waiting on you hand and foot, fetching and carrying, cleaning and scrubbing, you don't go wasting money on fancy slippers for her. She'd given me an old pair of Uncle Homer's boots and stuffed the toes with rags so's they wouldn't fall off. Frankly, they looked a sight smarter with my overalls than they had with my dresses.

Next I used my jackknife to hack off my braids. The blade was rusty and it hurt like the very dickens, but I managed to get my hair as short as a boy's.

The only thing I saved from my life as a girl was the locket hanging around my neck. Inside it were Mama's and Papa's pictures. As long as I kept the chain hidden under my shirt, nobody would see it.

Gathering up my dress, petticoat, and braids, I carried them to the railroad bridge just outside Clark Summit and tossed them over the edge. When my dress hit the water, it puffed up with air as though someone was still wearing it. I watched it float away taking my old self with it—an odd sensation but not altogether unpleasant.

"Good-bye, Eliza Yates," I whispered.

Though it was probably nothing but a muffled echo, I swear the river murmured, "Elijah Bates."

Elijah Bates—it was the perfect name for my new self. Enough like Eliza Yates to make it easy to remember, yet fit for a boy.

Repeating the name with every step, I ran across the bridge toward the Clark Summit train depot. Caesar raced ahead, looking back every now and then to make sure I was still behind him. That old dog didn't care what I called myself or what clothes I wore. Eliza Yates or Elijah Bates, I was the one he loved best in the whole wide world.

3

B Y THE TIME THE TICKET AGENT OPENED THE depot, the sun was just coming up. Caesar and I had been waiting on the platform for about two hours. To pass the time, we'd eaten all our food except an apple. Even though I was tuckered out from walking instead of sleeping, I was too excited to be tired. After all, this was the first day of my new life as Elijah Bates.

The ticket agent peered at me through his little window. "Well, well, you're up bright and early, sonny. What can I do for you today?"

I grinned when I heard him call me "sonny." Knowing I'd passed my first test, I shoved one of my gold coins under the grill. "I want a ticket on the first train heading west," I said, mimicking Little Homer's gruff voice.

The ticket agent studied the coin as if he thought it might be counterfeit. Raising his eyes but not his eyebrows, he frowned at me. "Where did you get this money, young man?"

I stared at him, guessing what he suspicioned. Lordy, he thought I'd stolen that ten dollars. "It's mine," I said, feeling my newfound confidence in my boyhood slip away.

The ticket agent slid the gold eagle round and round with one stubby finger. His nails were as dirty as if he'd spent the morning digging a hole in the earth with his bare hands.

"Well, now," he said thoughtfully, "I don't normally see raggedy boys with a ten-dollar gold piece in their pocket. Maybe you better take a seat over there while I send for the sheriff. Surely you won't mind cooling your heels till he gets hisself on over here. Not if this is really and truly your money."

I looked at the ticket agent. If the sheriff got involved in this, I was deader than dead. Who'd take the word of a child against a full-grown man like the ticket agent?

Reaching under the grill, I grabbed my money and ran.

"Come back here, boy!" the ticket agent hollered. I believe he meant to chase me but thought better of it when he saw Caesar.

"With that red hair, you won't get far!" he yelled. "I'll give your description to the sheriff, and he'll do up a poster with your face on it!"

Without looking back, I headed for the woods as

fast as I could go. Didn't slow down until I'd put at least a mile between Clark Summit and me. Even then I kept up a good pace. For all I knew, the sheriff had nothing better to do than chase after boys like me.

By late afternoon, I was hot and thirsty and hungry and tired. I'd never walked so far in Uncle Homer's big old boots. They were rubbing my heels raw. Finally I found a shady spot and flopped down in the grass, too weary to take another step. Hard as the ground was, it felt good to lie still.

Caesar collapsed beside me and panted in my face, not an altogether pleasant experience. I guess he was as hungry as I was, but all I had was the apple. When I showed it to him, he sniffed and turned his head away. I went ahead and ate it, but I swear I was hungrier after I'd finished it than I'd been before.

I lay in the grass, trying to ignore the ants crawling up and down my arms like I was their own private thoroughfare, and wondered what I should do next.

Overhead, thrushes were singing, showering me with music that fell like drops of gold from the treetops. Their song reminded me of a sad, sad story Mama once read to me. "The Babes in the Woods" it was called. It told of two poor children who lost their way in the wilderness. The birds took pity on them and covered their little bodies with leaves, but the children starved to death anyway.

Soon I began to think Caesar and I might end up like that boy and girl. We'd die here, and the birds would cover us. And then Papa would take it into his head to come back to Kansas. He'd be walking along this exact same trail and he'd stumble on my skeleton in the leaves, see the shiny locket round my neck, and know it was me, his own daughter, the child he'd abandoned so long ago.

Papa would gather the bones, not knowing, which were mine and which were Caesar's, and bury us together. Above our grave, he'd put a stone sculpture of a girl and a dog. The inscription would say HERE LIE POOR ELIZA YATES AND HER ONE AND ONLY FRIEND, CAESAR, A NOBLE DOG.

Thinking these thoughts made me so sad I cried myself to sleep. When I woke up, I was surprised to see the sun had set. Pink light lingered in the western sky, but the woods were darkening fast and the air was cold.

Belly empty, I shivered and got to my feet. At the same time, a gust of wind rustled the leaves overhead, bringing with it the smell of woodsmoke and beef stew. My stomach growled so loudly Caesar barked.

"Hush," I whispered. "We'll sneak over to the fire and see who's doing the cooking. If they look kindly, we'll ask if we can please have a bite."

Caesar and I crept through the trees and underbrush like Indians, scarcely making a sound. Not that it mattered much. The three men gathered around the campfire were raising such a ruckus they wouldn't have heard a runaway circus elephant on the rampage. As if whooping and hollering weren't enough, one of them fired a gun every now and then. The sound made their horses whinny and rear up. Startled the birds too, especially the crows roosting right over my head who added their caws to the racket.

It was plain to see the men weren't the kindly sort who'd share their food with a poor boy and his dog. The best thing to do was to wait until they fell asleep and then help ourselves to whatever was left in the pot.

Caesar and I hunkered down behind a big tree. The more the men drank, the louder they talked. The cuss words flew, too bad to repeat. If you're a poet of profanity, most likely you can imagine them for yourself.

When it was good and dark, a tall, skinny man with a face as flat as a shovel said, "Are we going to kill him or just leave him here to die on his own?"

For a second, I thought the man meant me, but before I gave myself away by begging for mercy, I realized some poor soul was lying on the ground on the other side of the fire. It was him they were talking about, not me.

The leader laughed the nastiest laugh I ever heard. "We got his money, his horse, and his gold watch. He ain't worth a bullet now."

"Don't forget he seen our faces, Roscoe," Shovel Face said. "If we don't kill him, he's bound to head straight for the sheriff's office. We're worth a lot of reward money."

Roscoe pulled out a pistol and looked at it like he was studying what to do. While he was deciding, he took a couple more swigs from a jug of whiskey.

Shovel Face started waving his pistol. "I swear if you don't kill him, I will. I ain't ready for the hanging tree." While he spoke, he listed to one side like gravity was pulling hard in that direction.

The third outlaw, a runty, bowlegged man with a bald head, was sitting on the ground watching. He'd look from Roscoe to Shovel Face and back again to Roscoe just like he was at a tennis game. Every now and then he hiccuped so hard his whole body shook. Then he'd giggle real high like a nervous girl.

Strangest of all, the man lying on the ground never said a word. Maybe he was asleep. I hoped he was. That way he wouldn't know when they shot him.

"If there's going to be any killing, I'm the one to do it." Roscoe pointed the gun at his chest, for emphasis I guess, and almost shot himself.

Staggering over to the man on the ground, he nudged him with his boot. "You got any last words, Featherbone?"

I leaned forward, hoping to see the doomed man's face, but it was too dark. I heard his answer, though.

"I wouldn't waste my precious breath on an ignorant lout such as yourself," he said.

Though the words he spoke were brave, Mr. Featherbone's voice quavered, making him sound like a boy playing a game of bluff with the school bully.

Roscoe scowled most fiercely and swore a long string of curses, most of them having to do with Mr. Featherbone's cheating ways. Then he aimed right at the poor man and pulled the trigger. The gun made a terrible sound, flashing fire and smoke. Mr. Featherbone cried out like the rabbit Little Homer once shot, a shrill, terrible sound I knew I'd recall to my dying day.

Forgetting myself, I screamed and hid my face, but the outlaws were too busy shouting and swearing to hear anything but themselves. Jumping on their horses, they galloped off into the dark, passing so close to my hiding place they nearly trampled me. They were riding so fast that Roscoe's old felt hat blew off. But he didn't stop to reclaim it.

For a long time Caesar and I stayed where we were, listening to the sound of the horses fade away into the night. When the woods were quiet again, I picked up Roscoe's hat, thinking it would make me look even more like a boy. Then I crawled a little closer to the campsite and peered through the bushes. The fire had burned down to glowing embers, but I could still smell the stew. It seemed being witness to a killing hadn't taken away my appetite.

The trouble was, I had to walk past Mr. Feather-bone to get to the stew. Till then the only dead person I'd ever seen was my poor, dear mama, and she'd been laid out neat and tidy in a coffin in the parlor. She'd gone peaceful, slipping out of her body as quiet as a butterfly leaving its cocoon. I was sad almost to dying myself, but I wasn't any more scared of Mama dead than I'd been scared of her alive.

Mr. Featherbone was a different case altogether. There hadn't been anything peaceful about his passing. From what I could tell, he'd been blown out of himself like a fish when you throw a stick of dynamite in a pond. If ever a dying man had left a vengeful spirit behind, it would be Mr. Feather-bone.

My empty stomach growled louder than ever, though. Desperate with hunger, I crept toward the fire, keeping my eyes on the stew pot so as not to see anything else. I bent down to get it, thinking I'd run as fast as I could once I had it in my hand. But just before I touched it, cold fingers wrapped around my ankle and a voice whispered, "For the Lord's sake, help me."

4

FOR THE FIRST TIME IN MY WHOLE LIFE I understood what people mean when they say their blood runs cold. Here I was just twelve years old, and a dead man had a hold of my ankle. I was frozen to the ground. Couldn't move. Couldn't cry out. Even Caesar seemed scared senseless. Didn't bark or growl. Just stood there with his tail between his legs, whimpering.

The dead man groaned, but he didn't let loose of me. "Help me, please," he whispered again.

I swallowed hard and looked down at Mr. Feather-bone. His face was mighty pale, and there was a powerful lot of blood dabbling his shirt, but he wasn't dead. What's more, he didn't appear to be more than seventeen years old. A boy, that's all he was. Curly haired, kind of thin, and delicate featured. What Aunt Mabel would call refined. Maybe even handsome.

Why, there was nothing to be scared of after all, except the blood—which was more than enough to make a squeamish girl like Millicent faint. Not me, though. Even before I became a boy, I wasn't the swooning type.

I knelt beside Featherbone. "I don't know a thing about bullet wounds," I admitted. "But if you tell me what to do, I'll help you. For surely you don't deserve to die."

He grimaced. "First bind my arm to stop the bleeding. Use the handkerchief in my coat pocket. Then clean the wound. There's a kettle of water by the fire."

Following his directions, I knotted the handkerchief around his left arm as tight as I dared and then washed the blood away. The poor fellow clenched his teeth, but every now and then a little moan slid out between them. I knew I was hurting him, but he made me keep on.

When I'd done all I could, Featherbone told me to go ahead and eat. Lying there on the ground, he looked pale but determined. The set of his jaw told me he didn't give up easy. He'd die when he was ready, I figured, and not one second before.

Taking care to give Caesar half, I gobbled the stew. The meat was tough and stringy, and the vegetables were mush, but I'd had fancy dinners at Aunt Mabel's table that I'd enjoyed far less.

When he'd eaten his share, Caesar gave a big

sigh of pure contentment and lay down by the fire. In no time he was sound asleep. But not me. I sat there, watching the flames flicker and thinking my own thoughts.

After a while, I glanced at Featherbone. He'd been so quiet I was afraid he might have upped and died on me after all. But he was wide awake, eyeing me with enough curiosity to kill a cat.

"A raggedy boy and a shaggy old dog," he said. "I don't know who you are or where you came from, but you most certainly saved my life."

"My name is Elijah." I drew out the syllables to savor the sound. "Elijah Yates."

"Elijah *what?*" Featherbone jerked upright and stared at me as if I'd just uttered the most terrible swear word ever invented.

"Elijah *Bates,*" I hollered, shocked to realize I'd said "Yates" instead of "Bates." "Bates, Bates, Bates. My name's Elijah *Bates.*"

Featherbone sighed and lay back. "Pardon me for startling you, but I could have sworn you said *Yates.* Thank the Lord you didn't. If there's one name in this world I despise, it's Yates."

I looked at him, alarmed by the hatred he was packing into my real name. "Did someone called Yates cause you grief?" I asked timidly.

"A dirty coward by that vile name shot my father in the back and left him to die in the street."

I drew in my breath so hard I almost choked. It

was a lucky thing I'd corrected myself and said my name was Bates. From the way Featherbone was carrying on, he might have killed me on the spot just because my name was Yates.

"I swore on my mother's grave I'd avenge my father's death," Featherbone went on, glaring at me as if I doubted his word. "I'm on my way to Tinville, Colorado, to confront the scoundrel."

"Why, that's just where I'm headed," I said, too surprised to keep my mouth shut as a more cautious person might have. Although I was sure Papa wasn't the kind to shoot a man in the back, it made me uneasy to know he and Featherbone's enemy not only were both named Yates but also lived in the same town. A coincidence no doubt, but worrisome all the same.

Featherbone stared at me, just as amazed as I was. "What in heaven's name takes an innocent child like you to a town as wicked as Tinville?" he asked.

"I hope to find my father there," I admitted.

Featherbone studied my face. "Aren't you rather young to be traveling by yourself?"

"I'm twelve years old," I said, drawing myself up to my full height. "Not that much younger than you, I reckon!"

"I'm almost eighteen," Featherbone said quickly. "Which makes me nearly a man and you a mere boy. Why, you should be at home with your mother, not roaming the countryside like a vagabond."

"My mama is dead," I whispered.

"So we're both motherless," Featherbone said, softening his haughty tone. "Orphan boys adrift in this cruel world with no place to call home."

When I turned my head to hide my tears, Featherbone touched my shoulder. "Allow me to introduce myself," he said. "I'm Calvin Thaddeus Featherbone, the Second." After pausing a moment, he added, "Perhaps you've heard of me."

"No," I apologized, "I'm afraid I haven't."

"In some parts," he said, watching me closely, "I'm known as the Gentleman Outlaw."

I stared at my companion, too awed to speak. Just a few days ago, I'd been an ordinary girl, doing chores and ducking whippings, and now here I was alone in the woods with a real, live outlaw. If he knew, my cousin Little Homer would be consumed with jealousy. He had a real hankering to become an outlaw himself, and if you ask me, he was already well on his way to achieving his goal.

"Are you telling me the honest-to-God truth?" I asked.

"Would I prevaricate, Elijah?"

Since I didn't know the meaning of the word, I ignored Calvin's question. "What did you do to become an outlaw?" I asked. "Rob a bank? Hold up a train?"

When Calvin didn't answer, I added, "I hope you didn't kill anybody. I don't approve of murder."

He stared into the fire, his face grim. Lord knows what he was thinking. "Never fear," he said at last. "I haven't taken anyone's life—yet."

Something in his voice made me shiver. Or maybe it was just the damp night air creeping up behind me. Swallowing hard, I said, "Are you aiming to kill the man who killed your daddy?"

Calvin clenched his jaw and nodded. "Yates showed no mercy to Father," he said. "I mean to show no mercy to him."

I moved a little closer to Caesar, taking comfort in his warm body and familiar smell. It seemed to me Calvin was studying my face with growing suspicion.

"Your father," he said slowly. "He wouldn't be the sheriff of Tinville, would he?"

"Sheriff?" I burst out laughing at the very idea of Papa being a sheriff. "Why, Aunt Mabel says Papa's about the worst man who ever lived. What makes you think he's a lawman?"

"The Yates I'm seeking is the sheriff of Tinville," Calvin said slowly, still staring into my eyes as if he hoped to read my mind like a carnival fortune-teller.

"I told you, Papa's name is *Bates*," I reminded him. "Even if his name was Yates—which it's not— he isn't the sort to wear a tin star."

After engaging me in a brief eye-to-eye stare, Calvin seemed to believe what I had told him. Yawning a yawn as big as a house, he stretched out on the ground. "If you'll pardon me, Eli, I shall endeavor to sink into the arms of Morpheus till morning."

I guess that meant Calvin aimed to go to sleep, because a few seconds later he was snoring as nice and polite as a lady in church.

But not me. I was too worried to shut my eyes. Much as I hated to part company with a famous outlaw, the sensible thing seemed to be to sneak away while Calvin slept. Go on to Tinville with Caesar. Find my father. Tell him he might have an enemy.

While I lay there trying to decide what to do, an owl hooted. Animals moved around in the bushes, rustling and snapping twigs. The sounds brought to mind the stories Little Homer made up to scare Millicent and William and me. What if the bogeyman was out there in the dark woods, waiting for me to leave the fire and come closer? The yellow-bellied snallygaster might be perched in a tree right over my head. The fierce turkey chatch that gobbled up little children could be hiding anywhere. I felt their red eyes watching me, smelled their evil smell, heard their sharp claws scratching in the dirt.

The owl called again, raising goose bumps on my skin. A few feet away, a branch snapped like something big and heavy had stepped on it. Moving even closer to Caesar, I hugged him tight. He whimpered and twitched like he was chasing rabbits in his dreams, but he didn't wake up.

I guessed I'd stay with Calvin a while. At least till daylight. Perhaps even longer. After all, we had miles to go before we got to Tinville. If by some weird quirk of fate it turned out Calvin and I were looking for the same man, I had plenty of time to sneak off and warn Papa.

Besides, I've never been one to do the sensible thing.

5

I F YOU'VE EVER HAD THE MISFORTUNE TO
spend a night sleeping on the cold ground without a blanket, you know how I felt when I woke up.
I was so blamed stiff I could hardly move. My mouth
tasted like I'd been chewing on Caesar's fur. Worst
of all, I had to hobble off into the trees and relieve
myself fast before Calvin noticed I wasn't exactly
who or what he thought I was.

By the time I came back, Calvin had gotten the
fire going, but nothing was cooking. It seemed the
Gentleman Outlaw wasn't the sort to hunt or fish or
carry supplies. He was accustomed to eating in
hotel dining rooms, he told me.

Caesar sighed and lay down beside the young
man. Calvin wrinkled his nose. "Pardon me for saying so," he said, "but this brute is badly in need of a
bath, Elijah."

"So are you," I said, making a great show of sniffing the air in Calvin's vicinity. It was true. After a night in the woods, the Gentleman Outlaw smelled a mite stale. I reckon I did too.

Ignoring me, Calvin attempted to move upwind from Caesar, but my loyal companion wagged his tail and moved closer.

"Why, Calvin," I said. "I believe Caesar likes you."

"Is that meant to be a compliment?"

"I reckon it is," I said, not sure whether I was pleased or jealous. "Caesar hates most everyone except me."

Calvin heaved a sigh and patted the dog. "It's my fate to be befriended by the lowest types, both animal and human," he said glumly.

Hoping he wasn't including me among the lowest types, I asked Calvin what he aimed to do next.

He shook his head. "This is a sad state of affairs for the Gentleman Outlaw," he said. "Thanks to Roscoe Suggs and his cronies, I have no money, no gun, and no horse. Those scoundrels relieved me of everything, including my watch and my playing cards."

"I've got some money," I said, hoping to cheer him.

Calvin raised his eyebrows hopefully. "How much?"

"I have two gold eagles in my pocket," I boasted, patting my overalls. "Twenty dollars is surely enough to get us on our way to Tinville."

Calvin's eyebrows drooped and his face took on a glum expression. "That's most generous of you, Elijah, but I fear twenty dollars won't even buy our passage out of Kansas."

Wishing I'd lied and said I had more, I watched Calvin get to his feet and take a couple of weak little steps, wincing and biting his lip. I jumped up so's he could lean on me. Caesar ran on ahead, pretending he knew just where we were going but looking back every now and then to make sure he was right.

By the time we reached the railroad tracks, Calvin was breathing hard. His shirt was soaked with sweat, and he was leaning on me heavier and heavier. It must have been about eight in the morning, but the sun was already hot. Gnats added to our discomfort by humming around our heads and nibbling on tender parts such as earlobes and eyelids.

"You want to sit and rest a spell?" I asked.

Calvin sank down in the weeds and leaned against a tree. His wound was bleeding again. I could see fresh red spreading across the old brown stains on his shirt sleeve.

"I can't take another step," he admitted. "Leave me here and go on toward Elms Bluff. It's that way." He gestured at a dirt road snaking off along the river and then continued in a voice so low I had to lean close to hear him. "When you come to a little yellow house at the top of a hill, ask for Nellie. Tell her I'm in need of help. She'll know what to do."

With that, he closed his eyes as if he were too tired to say another word.

I fanned him with the hat Roscoe had left behind, but Calvin didn't move. "You look mighty poorly," I whispered.

"That's odd," he mumbled. "I feel mighty poorly."

"You aren't fixing to die, are you?"

"Not if I can help it." Calvin opened those blue eyes of his for a second. "Go on, Elijah. Fetch Miss Nellie."

I hated to leave Calvin there all by his lonesome, so I persuaded Caesar to stay with him. "Keep him safe," I told my dog. "Don't let anyone come near him."

Caesar nodded like he understood, and I took off, fearing for Calvin's life.

By the time I spotted the tumbledown yellow house, I felt like I'd been running and walking, running and walking, for hours. I was glad to see two ladies sitting on the doorstep, fanning themselves. One had long blond hair, and the other had jet black hair done up on top of her head. Frankly, neither color looked natural. Nor did their pink cheeks. Their dresses seemed mighty small somehow, like they'd grown since they'd bought them and could scarcely get the buttons fastened.

Never having seen ladies like this, I stared so hard they smiled and waved at me.

"Hey, there," the blonde called. "What are you looking at, boy?"

The other laughed, showing a mouthful of gold teeth. "Take a picture, why don't you? It'll last a sight longer."

I was dying of mortification, but I walked up to them even though I knew full well they weren't proper churchgoing ladies. No, sir. They were the kind the preacher talked against on long, hot Sundays. Aunt Mabel wouldn't have gone anywhere near them—which gave me a certain amount of pleasure.

"Is one of you Miss Nellie?" I asked.

The blonde tossed her hair. "Who wants to know?"

"Calvin Featherbone sent me to fetch you," I said. "He's hurt bad."

Miss Nellie jumped up and pressed her hand to her heart, which you could almost see beating on account of her dress being cut so low. "Oh, I just knowed Calvin was going to get hisself in trouble," she cried. "I told him to stay clear of that low-down scum Roscoe. Didn't I, Pearl?"

"You surely did, honey." Miss Pearl heaved herself up beside Miss Nellie and laid a big soft white hand on my shoulder. "Where is the poor young man?"

"In a grove of trees beside the train tracks, about two miles from here. He can't walk all this way. Can you fetch him in a buggy?"

Miss Pearl nodded real solemn-like and turned to Miss Nellie. "Harness up Fancy. While you're gone, I'll heat some water."

I followed Miss Nellie around back to the stable. A sorry-looking old gray horse raised up its head and looked down its nose at me. I swear its teeth were worn down worse than Miss Pearl's.

"Give me a hand with the harness, boy," said Miss Nellie.

Between the two of us, we were on the road in just a few minutes, which was a good thing because that horse wasn't going to get us to Calvin any sooner than if we'd walked.

"How bad is Calvin hurt?" Miss Nellie asked.

"Mr. Roscoe Suggs shot him in the left arm. I reckon he was aiming for his heart but he was too drunk to shoot straight."

"I warned Calvin not to cheat Roscoe, I begged him, but would that boy listen to me? No, sir, he would not." Miss Nellie flicked the reins so hard they stung the horse's back. "Some folks think they know it all, but talking like you swallowed a dictionary don't mean a thing if you ain't got any common sense."

Miss Nellie went on in that vein, working herself up into a real temper. If she was to be believed, the Gentleman Outlaw had a lot to learn. Some of what she said I agreed with. I'd already noticed Calvin's snobby airs and fancy words, but I hoped he wasn't as foolish as she thought he was.

"Now he's probably up and died on me," Miss Nellie said, "which is just the sort of selfish thing he'd do. No consideration for anybody. Probably expects me to pay for his burial too."

By now Miss Nellie was crying. Tears ran down her cheeks, leaving little tracks in her pink powder. "Oh, that Calvin Featherbone," she sobbed. "I wish to heaven I'd never seen his face."

Finally we came over the crest of a hill and saw Calvin lying under the tree where I'd left him. Caesar sat beside him, keeping watch like a good dog.

When he caught sight of Miss Nellie and me, the Gentleman Outlaw raised his head and made a sort of grimace meant to be a smile. "What took you so confounded long?" he asked. "I'm astonished I lived to see you again."

Miss Nellie didn't say a word, not even an "I told you so." She just gathered Calvin up, hurt arm and all, and kissed him till he begged her to let loose of him. He said it fancier, of course, but that was the gist of it.

With me on one side and Miss Nellie on the other, we got Calvin into the buggy. Caesar lay down beside him, and I took my seat next to Miss Nellie. Back to the little yellow house we went, slow and easy, trying not to jostle Calvin.

Miss Pearl was waiting for us on the steps. She and Miss Nellie helped Calvin inside and laid him on a bed. While I watched with a kind of horrified fascination, they started peeling the handkerchief off Calvin's arm. I knew it hurt, but he didn't whimper, just clenched his teeth till his jaw nearly busted.

"Looks like it's infected," Miss Pearl said. "Fetch the hot water, Nellie. I'll be needing clean rags, too, and some of my remedies."

Turning to me, Miss Pearl added, "You go on outside and wait. We don't want no boy nor his dog in here getting in the way."

While Miss Nellie and Miss Pearl worked on Calvin, I sat on the old splintery steps and watched the afternoon shadows creep toward the house. The closer they got, the cooler it felt. Seemed like the earth didn't hold May sunshine long.

After a while, Miss Pearl came out and took a seat beside me. "That's a nice dog you got," she said.

I looked at Caesar. He was lying beside me, his head on my knee, slobbering on my overalls, just as happy as he could be. "He's not half-bad," I admitted, but it wasn't Caesar I was interested in talking about. "How's Calvin feeling, ma'am?"

"Oh, I 'spect he'll live till the next time somebody takes a shot at him."

Miss Pearl sighed and patted my head. "Lordy, boy, your hair's a sight. Looks like somebody hacked it off with a dull knife. You come inside and let me barber it nice for you."

Next thing I knew Miss Pearl had me in a chair

with an apron tied round my neck. *Clip clippety clip. Snip snippety snip.* In no time at all, the floor around me was covered with little red ringlets coiled tight as watch springs.

Miss Pearl looked at them. "It's a shame to waste such pretty curls on a boy," she said.

I kept my head down so's she wouldn't see the flush creeping over my skin. It made me nervous having her so close. Surely something would give me away and she'd see I was a girl.

"What's this?" Just as I feared, she'd found the locket under my shirt.

I tried to snatch it away, but Miss Pearl was too fast. In a flash, she had the locket open and was staring at Mama's and Papa's tiny faces.

"It's all I got left of my folks," I whispered. "I wear it close to my heart to keep it safe."

Miss Pearl shut the locket and let me slide it under my shirt again. "Poor little lamb," she said softly. "Are you alone in this world?"

"Mama's been dead for nigh onto five years, but Papa's prospecting for silver and gold in Colorado. That's where I'm bound."

"Ain't nobody getting rich mining nowadays," said Miss Pearl. "Your pa done missed the good years."

I shrugged. "I don't care whether he's rich or poor, just so long as I find him."

Miss Pearl nodded as if she understood. Picking

up a broom, she started sweeping my curls onto a sheet of newspaper. The headline caught my eye: DISAPPEARANCE ENDS IN TRAGEDY. Squinting hard, I made out my own name as well as Homer and Mabel Watkins's, but the print was too small to read the details.

I guess Miss Pearl saw what I was staring at, because she got a melancholy look on her face. Stooping down, she picked up the paper and handed it to me.

"That's the saddest thing I ever heard tell of," she said. "This poor little old girl disappeared from her home over to Bartlett. Yesterday some fishermen found her dress in the river not far from here. No sign of her body yet, but the sheriff's calling it murder."

Miss Pearl wiped a tear away. "Eliza Yates was an orphan, poor thing, but unlike you and me, she had kind and loving relatives to look after her. Their hearts are just plain broke."

You can bet I was busting to set Miss Pearl straight about those poor grieving relatives. In fact, I had to bite my tongue to keep quiet.

Miss Pearl sighed and swept up the last curl. "Just 'cause you're a boy, don't think you're safe," she said. "There's a lot of wickedness in this old world."

When she wasn't looking, I slipped the paper into my overalls pocket, hoping to keep Calvin from reading about Eliza Yates. No telling what ideas *her* name might give him about *my* name.

But Calvin wasn't the only reason I wanted that paper. It's not every day a girl gets to read the story of her own death.

W HEN SHE WAS SATISFIED WITH MY APPEAR-
ance, Miss Pearl handed me Roscoe's old hat,
kissed me on the nose, and sent Caesar and me out
to the stable. "Nellie's got Calvin hid away in the
hay," she said. "We'll bring you some supper later,·
but you stay put. There's no telling what kind of
company we'll get tonight. If Roscoe was to show
up—"

She didn't have to say another word. Caesar and
I hightailed it to the stable, where we found Calvin
taking his ease.

"Well, well," he said, clapping eyes on my haircut.
"Aren't you the dandy, Elijah."

"You look a sight perkier yourself," I said, flop-
ping down beside him. Miss Nellie had found him a
clean shirt and put his arm in a sling. Although he
was still shadowy around the eyes, he'd gotten some
color in his cheeks.

"Nellie and Pearl are of the opinion I'll live," Calvin said.

"When do they think you'll be fit to travel?"

"In a week or two." Calvin yawned. "Rest is what I need," he said, closing his eyes. "I lost a copious amount of blood, you know."

Taking the hint, I rolled over on my back and let myself sink into the soft hay. The sun came through the stable door slantwise and warmed my face. Dust motes danced in shafts of light. Birds sang in the woods. Nearby, Caesar scratched his fleas. It wasn't often either one of us had a chance to lie still and do nothing. I decided to enjoy it as long as I could.

→>•◄←

As it turned out, we ended up spending a little less than two weeks with Miss Pearl and Miss Nellie. During that time, I had plenty to eat and no work to do. No cross words or beatings either. Little Homer would have thrown a fit if he'd seen me lounging by the creek with a fishing rod or roaming through the woods picking blueberries for one of Miss Pearl's pies. I was leading the ideal boy's life and loving every minute of it.

At night I'd nestle down in the hay near Calvin and ask him questions about his past. Bit by bit, I pieced together his life story. Though he spun the tale in long fancy words and complicated sentences, this was the gist of it.

Long before Calvin himself was born, his daddy owned a plantation in Maryland. When the Civil War broke out, Mr. Calvin Thaddeus Featherbone, Senior, joined the Confederate Army, which riled me somewhat as my daddy fought for the Union. In fact, it was all I could do to keep from calling Mr. Featherbone a dirty low-down traitor. Even though it's all water under the bridge now, folks in Kansas don't have much love for rebels. We suffered a great deal at their hands.

Anyhow, when Calvin's daddy came home from the war, he found his plantation in ruins. The slaves had run off (hooray for them) and the crops hadn't been planted and the house was in sorry shape because the Union troops had used it for their headquarters, resulting in much of it being blown up by the rebels. Mr. Featherbone tried to farm his land himself but he soon went broke, as he'd never done any hard work before, poor man.

For a while, Calvin's granddaddy helped out. He was a rich man, a millionaire, Calvin claimed, who lived in a big fancy mansion in Baltimore. Trouble was, he hadn't wanted his daughter to marry Calvin Thaddeus Featherbone, Senior. Thought he was a lazy, no-account southern sympathizer, which led to bad feelings all around.

Not long after Calvin was born, Mr. Featherbone got fed up with taking charity from a man who despised him. Leaving his wife and son behind, he headed west just as my daddy had done. He soon discovered gambling was an easier way to get rich than prospecting. If Calvin could be believed, Mr. Featherbone, Senior, was Doc Holliday's equal, good at cards and good at shooting but always a perfect gentleman—like Calvin himself.

Sad to say, just as he was about to make a real name for himself, Mr. Featherbone had the misfortune to get killed by the sheriff of Tinville. When the news came, Calvin's mother made her son promise to avenge his daddy's death. Then she died herself. Of a broken heart, I reckon.

Three months before I met him, Calvin had left Maryland, dressed in expensive clothes and riding a fine black horse. He was heading west with some of his grandfather's money in his pocket, a silver-handled pistol in his belt, and revenge in his heart. But through a series of misfortunes, Calvin ended up losing everything except the revenge in his heart.

"Ambushed, robbed, and left for dead by a trio of inept scoundrels," he summed up his story one night. "Rescued by a twelve-year-old boy and nursed back to health by a pair of good-hearted ladies. I'm a disgrace to my father's memory."

"But you're an outlaw," I reminded him. "Surely you can get rich again by robbing a bank or holding up a train."

Calvin shook his head. "A fine outlaw I am. No gun, no horse, and no money to purchase either."

So saying, he rolled himself up in his blanket, turned his back on me, and fell asleep.

-->-•-<-+-

The very next morning, Miss Pearl sat us down at the kitchen table and said she didn't know how much longer she could keep feeding us. "Times are tough, Calvin. It's getting harder and harder to earn a living the way the new sheriff's carrying on, but I'm willing to keep the boy if he wants to stay."

She gave me a big grin that showed all her gold teeth. "I'll make sure you get enough to eat, Eli. You and your dog both."

Much as I appreciated Miss Pearl's generosity, I spoke up fast. "Thank you kindly, but I'll go with Calvin. I have to find my father, you know."

"Fathers," Miss Pearl muttered, heading for the kitchen. "I swear they cause more trouble and heartbreak than anything else in this miserable world."

Miss Nellie turned to Calvin, her pretty face screwed up with worry. "Are you still planning to hunt that sheriff down?"

"Of course I am," Calvin said.

"Oh, Lord," Miss Nellie cried. "You can't even defend yourself against a drunken no-account bum like Roscoe Suggs. How do you expect to take on a lawman?"

Calvin's face flushed with anger. "You underestimate me, Nell! That cowardly Suggs lay in wait and took me by surprise. It will be a different matter when I step off the train in Tinville. I'll have the upper hand there, not Yates."

"I swear you're just bound and determined to get yourself killed," Miss Nellie said. Without looking at Calvin again, she burst into tears and ran from the room.

Calvin went after her, but I stayed at the table, too worried to move. Miss Nellie's words hung in the air like a bothersome echo. I hoped she was wrong about the Gentleman Outlaw. I didn't want to see him killed in Tinville any more than she did.

After a long while, Calvin came back to the table, but Miss Nellie stayed in her room. Even with the door shut, I could hear her crying.

"Are we leaving now?" I asked.

Instead of answering, Calvin drummed his fingers on the table, glancing at me every now and then like he had something on his mind. The longer he sat there, the uneasier I got. If Miss Pearl hadn't been making such a ruckus washing dishes, I'd have gone to the kitchen just to get away from Calvin, but I reckoned she was in a bad mood and might put me to work scrubbing pots.

At last Calvin spoke. "How much money did you say you have, Elijah?"

"Twenty dollars."

Calvin held out his hand. "Let me see it."

When I hesitated, he reached across the table and pulled a gold coin out of my ear. "My, my," he said. "Look what I found."

Before I could wiggle away from him, Calvin pretended to find a second coin in my other ear. It was an old trick I'd seen dozens of times at the fair, but Calvin was so good I almost believed the coins were really in my ears and not hidden in his fingers.

I reached into my overalls pocket and felt for my precious gold eagles. They were gone. "Hey," I shouted, grabbing for the coins, but Calvin was too fast for me. Sliding my money into his pockets, he got to his feet.

"Come along," he said. "It's time we departed."

"Give me my money!" I hollered. "That's my twenty dollars, the one thing in this world Mama left me!"

Calvin looked me in the eye. "If we are to travel together, we must share and share alike. No mine. No yours. Just *ours*. Our money."

"How come the money has to be in *your* pocket?" I asked. "Why can't it be in *my* pocket?"

"Because I'm older than you," Calvin said. "Bigger, too. And a great deal smarter." He jingled the coins and smiled. "Don't fret. I'll take good care of your inheritance. Before I'm done, we'll be as rich as kings."

"Don't you believe him, Eli," Miss Pearl called from the kitchen.

The Gentleman Outlaw spun around to face her.

"Why, Pearl, the next time you see me, I'll be riding a fine horse and wearing a proper gentleman's clothing."

"I won't hold my breath," said Miss Pearl. "And, Eli, you better not hold yours either. Calvin's a fine one for promising the moon and coming up with a handful of dust."

As Calvin headed for the door, I followed close at his heels. Like Miss Pearl, I knew better than to believe in promises. I wasn't planning to let Calvin Featherbone out of my sight. Not while he had my money.

7

HOURS LATER, CALVIN AND I WERE BUMPING along a dusty road in Miss Pearl's buggy. Just before we left her place, she'd had a softening of the heart. We could borrow the buggy and Fancy as long as we promised to leave them at a certain livery stable in Dodge City. The owner would be happy to drive them back to her, Miss Pearl said, flashing those gold teeth one last time.

When I'd asked Calvin why we couldn't get on the train in Elms Bluff, he'd said he had too many enemies in these parts, including the sheriff. They'd be sure to watch for him at the depot. That was why we were skedaddling under cover of darkness, like true wanted men.

As we passed through woods and fields, I could scarcely believe I was traveling with a genuine outlaw. Train robberies, bank holdups, shoot-outs with sheriffs, wild Indians—why, there was just no telling what dangers lay ahead for Calvin and me.

Even Caesar seemed to sense something exciting was about to begin. He lunged around in the back of the buggy, sniffing the night air and barking every now and again as if he could barely wait to get wherever it was we were going.

I nudged Calvin. "Can I have a name like yours?"

"Surely you don't want to change *Bates* to *Featherbone.*"

"No," I said, giggling at the idea of having a name as silly as Featherbone. "I'm talking about an outlaw name. You know what I mean—the sort you see on wanted posters."

Calvin chuckled. "Why, you can give yourself any sobriquet you like, Eli."

Sobriquet—I mouthed the word silently, enjoying its sound. To Calvin I said, "My sobriquet is Kid Bates. If we hold up any banks, that's what I want you to call me."

Calvin nodded. "The Gentleman Outlaw and his accomplice, Kid Bates. Yes, that will do nicely."

"We might rob a bank or hold up a train," I said, "but we won't kill anyone."

"Not unless we have to," Calvin agreed.

"And we'll share our loot with the poor unfortunates of this world," I added.

Calvin sighed. "I doubt we'll meet anyone more poor and unfortunate than ourselves."

I studied his face to see if he was pulling my leg, but his features were hard to read. "The James brothers always gave to the needy," I reminded him. "I heard they once saved a widow's farm by paying off her mortgage."

Calvin nodded. "I've heard that story," he said. "Frank and Jesse held up the bank the very next day and stole the money back."

"Yes, but the widow kept her farm."

Calvin had no more to say on the subject, so we rode along for a while without talking. The moon came with us, turning the dusty road to a chalky white barred with black shadows. On either side, the woods were dark and still. There wasn't a house in sight nor any sign of a human being. Frogs peeped and thrummed. The wind whispered in the leaves, and an owl hooted. It was a lonely place.

Calvin slowed the horse and peered into the shadows ahead. "It was in a spot like this that Roscoe and his boys ambushed me," he muttered.

I shivered and drew a little closer to him. "What did you do to make those men hate you so?"

"Quite simply, I won their money in a game of cards. Poor losers, that's what they were."

"Miss Nellie told me you cheated Roscoe. She begged you not to, but you wouldn't listen to her."

"Nell said I cheated?" Calvin turned up his nose. "The very idea. I merely used a few tricks my father taught me."

"But aren't tricks the same as cheating?"

"Certainly not," Calvin said. "My father was a man among men. He didn't need to cheat to win."

Without looking at me again, Calvin flicked the

reins to remind Fancy she was supposed to be pulling the buggy, not eating honeysuckle, and we moved on, bouncing and swaying over the ruts in the road. Lulled by the rocking motion, I fell asleep with my head resting on Calvin's shoulder.

→>•◂←

When I woke up, the sun was just starting to creep above the horizon. Calvin estimated we'd put twenty miles between us and Elms Bluff, but it was at least another day's ride to Dodge City. Turning Fancy off the road, he found a nice stopping place in a grove of trees.

"You and Caesar slept for hours," he said, "but poor old Fancy and I have been awake all night."

We ate the food Miss Nellie had packed for us, and then Calvin lay down in the buggy and fell fast asleep, leaving me to entertain myself with my own thoughts, which tended to center around my future exploits as Kid Bates.

After a while, I got out my harmonica and went through my repertoire, which consisted of songs like "The Old Folks at Home," "Jeannie with the Light Brown Hair," and "Home Sweet Home." They were mostly sad and mournful tunes, the kind that sound best on a harmonica, which makes music just about as lonesome as a train whistle late at night and far away.

While I played, Caesar lay at my feet. Sometimes

he accompanied me with a soft whimpery howl, but for the most part he was content to look pitiful and sigh now and then in a melancholy way.

When I stopped to get a drink of water, I saw Calvin sitting up in the buggy, watching me. I started to apologize, thinking he was mad because I'd waked him, but he jumped down from the seat in good spirits and slapped me on the back.

"That was fine playing, Eli," he said. "You and that wretched dog could wring tears out of the hardest heart—and silver as well."

I looked at him. "What do you mean?"

"We'll go into the next town and pick a nice spot where you can play your harmonica," he said. "If we're fortunate, passersby will take pity on you, a poor orphan boy."

"Are you asking me to stand on a corner and beg?" I felt my face heat up like my brain was about to explode. "There's no way on God's green earth I'll do something that shameful!"

Calvin's good-natured grin disappeared as if somebody had wiped it off with a rag. "We have twenty dollars to our name," he said. "How far do you suppose that will get us?"

I didn't rightly know, so I didn't answer. Nor did I look into those blue eyes of his. I just stood there, scuffing at the dust with the toe of my old boot.

"Are you going to allow pride to stand between you and finding your father?"

Calvin's voice had softened a bit, but I wasn't

about to surrender without a fight. "Why can't we hold up a bank or a train instead? We'd get us a sight more money."

"Must I remind you again? I have neither a gun nor the money to purchase one."

"That wouldn't stop a man like your father," I said. "He wouldn't make a kid beg for him. No, sir, he'd find some other way to get money."

For a moment I thought Calvin was going to haul off and hit me, but he controlled his temper. Turning his back, he climbed onto the buggy seat, clucked to Fancy, and asked me if I was coming or not.

I scrambled up beside him. "Since you have my twenty dollars," I muttered, "it seems I got no choice."

"Smart boy," said Calvin, showing off a set of teeth Doc Holliday would have been pleased to see if he decided to take up dentistry again.

And that was that. As usual, Calvin had gotten his way. Off we went, with Caesar trailing behind, leaving his mark on as much of Kansas as he could.

8

I N THE AFTERNOON WE CAME TO A GOOD-SIZED
town with wide, dusty streets. It boasted a new
church, a schoolhouse, a handsome bank, a goodly
number of business establishments, and a fine
selection of homes, some more respectable than
others. The wood sidewalks were crowded with folks
going about their Saturday shopping, and the
streets were full of horses and wagons.

Calvin picked a nice shady spot across from the
bank. "Lay your hat on the ground," he said, "and
play soft and sweet, Eli. Look as sad and lonesome
as you can. If folks ask, tell them you're a poor
orphan child with no one to love or cherish you."

Calvin paused to study Caesar who lay beside me,
his head on my shoe, his eyes as sorrowful as a hungry dog's can be.

"Perfect," he said. "Some folks will feel sorry for
you, but others will pity Caesar. Frankly, if given a

choice, many people would rather see a human die than an animal."

With that, Calvin walked off and left me. He had business of his own to tend to, he said.

I watched him disappear, sidestepping piles of horse dung in the street as dainty as a fancy dancer. Then I raised my harmonica to my lips and began to play "Home Sweet Home." It wasn't hard to act the part of a lone, lorn orphan. In fact, I just had to be myself.

Before long, a pretty lady in a red dress tossed a penny in my hat. Soon I had ten coins, then too many to count. Inspired by my success, I began to branch out and play hymns from church. *Clink clink clink* went pennies and nickels and even a silver dollar from a gent carrying a gold-headed cane.

Some folks asked me questions and clucked their tongues when I told them I was an orphan. Others worried about Caesar. Was he getting enough to eat? Was I treating him right? One lady actually went into a nearby butcher shop and came out with a bone for him. An old man brought him a bucket of water. I couldn't help noticing nobody gave me a thing to eat or drink. Which led me to believe Calvin was right about folks pitying animals more than people.

Every now and then one or two passersby would pause nearby and chat for a while. More than once I heard them speak of the poor orphan girl who was murdered so cruelly in Bartlett. It surprised me to know my fame had spread so far, but I learned right quick to play the saddest songs of all when I heard my name. Eliza Yates's dreadful fate reminded folks of me. Here was a living orphan they could help. It tickled me to profit from my own death.

After an hour or so, a gentleman wearing a top hat and a look that matched came up to me and said, "We don't take kindly to beggars here. Move along, you wretched little miscreant. And take that pathetic excuse for a dog with you before I get a notion to shoot him as a public nuisance."

Just as I was about to be run out of town, the Gentleman Outlaw came strolling around the corner. He took one look and doffed his hat to the important gentleman.

"Good afternoon, sir," he said with all the politeness a body could want. "I see you've found my poor little orphan brother for whom I've been searching."

Calvin reached for me. In so doing, he tripped over Caesar, lost his balance, and fell against the important gentleman. After apologizing profusely, he turned to me, still acting weak and wobbly. "I know you wanted to help, Elijah, but I'd rather be dead of this plagued consumption than see you beg for our daily bread."

I stared at Calvin, too surprised to speak, but he leaned against me, coughing into his handkerchief as if he'd left his deathbed to find me. Never had I seen a more piteous sight. If I hadn't known better, I'd have thought he was about to expire in my arms.

By now a goodly crowd had gathered, many of whom had helped fill my hat with coins. It was plain to see where their sympathy lay, but the important gentleman was too puffed up with pride to notice.

"What your brother needs is a good flogging," said he, twirling his mustache like a regular villain.

"Indeed, sir, I'll make sure Elijah doesn't bother you again," Calvin said with mock humility. Turning to me, he told me to pick up my hat before someone tripped over it.

While I stood there, clutching the hat to my chest, Calvin returned his attention to the important gentleman.

"Please accept my apologies for offending your sensibilities, sir. I realize that respectable citizens such as yourself prefer us unfortunates to suffer and die out of sight, sir."

The important gentleman glanced around uneasily, as if he was just beginning to notice the mood of the crowd. "It's high time you both moved along," he said, not sounding quite as sure of himself as before.

"Yes, sir," Calvin said. "it's high time, high time indeed." With a tip of his hat, he led me away, still leaning on my shoulder and coughing dramatically.

Behind us, the crowd hooted and jeered at the

important gentleman. The last I saw of him he was striding toward the bank, swinging his cane and doing his best to ignore the children parading along behind him mimicking every step he took.

After a few minutes, Calvin ducked into an alley between two shops. Twirling a gold pocket watch in my face, he said, "Yes, sir, it's high time, Eli, high time indeed."

"Where in tarnation did you get that?"

Calvin gave me a scornful look. "Where do you think?"

"You stole it from the gentleman."

"'Stole' is a harsh word, Elijah. As for 'gentleman'—well, I wouldn't honor that rogue with such a fine appellation. Flog you indeed. The very idea. If I weren't dying of consumption, I'd flog *him*."

Calvin examined the watch and dropped it into his pants pocket. "Not very good quality, I fear, but I suppose it will do for now."

I stared at him, speechless. I knew he robbed banks and trains and such. But to think he was also a common pickpocket was a mite disappointing.

"You look rather glum, Eli."

Calvin had read my mind, just as if the thoughts I was thinking were written on my forehead for him to see. "Well," I admitted, "somehow it doesn't seem very sporting to snatch a gentleman's watch without even telling him."

Leaning closer so we were eyeball to eyeball,

Calvin said, "Consider this, Elijah Bates. I didn't hurt him or kill him, and no one could fault my manners."

"I don't recall you thanking him for the watch."

Calvin laughed. "You're a clever lad, Eli." Taking the hat from me, he counted the coins. It seemed I'd gotten a total of three dollars and forty-seven cents, plus a shiny silver button and a fine-looking agate shooting marble. Not bad for an hour's work, I guess, but nothing to be proud of.

After pocketing the money, Calvin leaned against the wall, thinking hard, judging from the looks of the wrinkles in his forehead.

I held out my hand. "Don't I get some of that?"

Absentmindedly, Calvin dropped the marble and the button into my palm and went on thinking.

I took them, but I was far from satisfied. "I earned every cent of that money, Calvin, but I'll be happy to split it fifty-fifty."

He looked at me then. "As I said before, I'll take care of the financial end of our ventures, Eli."

I shoved my palm under his nose. "I want my share. And I want it now!"

"What a stubborn little rogue you are." Slowly he reached into his pocket and pulled out a handful of change. Counting carefully, he gave me twenty cents.

"Go buy yourself some candy and a sarsaparilla and whatever else your little heart desires," he said in a kindlier voice. "I have a bit more thinking to do."

Leaving Calvin to his thoughts and Caesar to his fleas, I ducked and dodged my way across the street and into a store.

I suppose twenty cents was a cheap bribe, but I have a powerful craving for sweets. Aunt Mabel was in the habit of giving Millicent, William, and Little Homer all the candy they wanted, but when it came to me, she said it might ruin my teeth. She wasn't about to pay to have a dentist pull them out. So I got to sit there and watch my three cousins slurp and sneer their way through peppermint sticks and licorice and jawbreakers as big as baseballs.

Now it was my turn. I bought a bottle of sarsaparilla and so much candy it filled two bags.

When I got back, Calvin was standing where I'd left him, still lost in thought, but Caesar had given up on his fleas and fallen asleep. I offered Calvin a swallow of sarsaparilla and a peppermint drop, but he shook his head. Since he didn't seem to be in a talkative mood, I squatted beside him and went to work on a long sticky string of red licorice.

In all my twelve years on this earth, I couldn't recall being happier. No beatings and scoldings. No chores. No Uncle Homer and Aunt Mabel. No Little Homer, Millicent, and William. All the candy my belly could hold.

Begging seemed a small price to pay for such freedom.

C ALVIN AND I SPENT THE NEXT FEW DAYS going from town to town, me begging and him collecting my earnings. I can't say I enjoyed it, but as I said, I'd done far worse things—cleaning the outhouse, for instance. It also helped to remind me that every penny in my hat was bringing me closer to finding Papa.

Along the way, I taught Caesar some new tricks. In addition to shaking hands, he could now beg, play dead, and dance on his hind legs when I played lively songs such as "Yankee Doodle Went to Town" or "O, Susanna!" His antics boosted my earnings considerably.

By the time I'd increased our fortune to seventy dollars, I thought we had plenty to buy two tickets to Tinville, but Calvin was itching to try his luck at the gambling tables in Dodge City. His father had written a long letter describing the town as wide open, lawless, and wild. You could get away with anything in the "Beautiful, Bibulous Babylon of the Plains," a nickname Calvin liked the sound of. He said it was a fine example of alliteration, whatever that meant.

Of course, Calvin's father said you had to observe certain niceties even in Dodge. You never shot an unarmed man, for instance. Never stole a horse unless you wanted to hang for it. Never insulted a lady. Or cheated a widow or an orphan. Other than that, you could pretty much do what you pleased and the devil take you.

As exciting as the town sounded, I hoped Calvin didn't intend to stay more than a couple of days. We'd already spent much too much time dillydallying across Kansas, I thought.

But when I asked Calvin how soon we'd be leaving for Tinville, he said, "Not until we can afford first-class tickets. I intend to arrive in style, Eli, so as to make an impression on Sheriff Yates. He must see I'm a man to be reckoned with."

The sound of my true name always made me uncomfortable, so I fell silent. Not that Calvin noticed. He was so busy talking about his grand entrance that he probably wouldn't have noticed if I'd fallen off the buggy.

"I'll step from the train, holding my head high," he went on. "I'll be wearing a fine black frock coat, made of the best wool and custom-tailored. Under it, an embroidered vest and a lacy shirt with a diamond stickpin. I'll have diamonds on my fingers, too. Trousers cut just right. Shiny black boots."

I glanced at Calvin. He was wearing a shabby black jacket and baggy pants with a tear in the knee. His white shirt was frayed at the collar, and his boots were almost as scuffed as mine. He needed a shave and a haircut. At the moment, Calvin Featherbone was far from the dandy he hoped to become.

But Calvin wasn't the sort to let the truth get in the way of dreams. No, sir, not him. He kept right on spouting foolishness. "Someone in the crowd at the depot will notice me," he said. "He'll run to the sheriff and tell him a dangerous man has arrived in Tinville."

Though I'd said nothing, Calvin scowled at me as if he thought I doubted him. "My showdown with Sheriff Yates will make the gunfight at the O.K. Corral resemble a Sunday school picnic," he boasted.

Apparently satisfied he'd convinced me, Calvin urged Fancy to get a move on. Way far off, on the edge of the world, we could just make out a tiny huddle of buildings against the sky. It was Dodge City, Calvin assured me, the queen of the cow towns.

→>•<←

We reached the outskirts of Dodge just before sunset. To my surprise, it looked as peaceful and ordinary as any other town. Houses and churches and schools, folks out strolling, pigs and chickens making themselves comfortable in the dust. Not a sign of a drunken cowboy or a herd of longhorns. No shooting either. Few saloons.

By the time we found the livery stable, Calvin was looking a bit down in the mouth.

The man who knew Miss Pearl was right pleased to see us—and the horse.

"Pearl wrote that you were coming," Mr. Sullivan said. "But I expected you sooner." He was a rough-looking fellow with a shaggy mustache and a bushy beard. I believe a scowl was his natural expression.

Calvin didn't offer Mr. Sullivan any excuses. What he wanted to know was why the town was so quiet. "I anticipated a lively scene," he said, frowning as if Mr. Sullivan were somehow to blame for the boarded-up saloons we'd passed on Front Street.

Mr. Sullivan laughed out loud. "Why, where in tarnation have you been? The cattle don't come here no more and neither do the cowboys. Without them, there wasn't no need for gamblers and saloonkeepers and dance-hall girls, so they packed up and followed the railroad west. In their place, we got teachers, preachers, lawyers, bankers, doctors, and storekeepers. You know what kind of folks men of that sort bring with them."

Here Mr. Sullivan spat in the dust at my feet. "Self-righteous folks," he said. "Churchgoing folks.

Teetotaling folks. Folks with wives and little children. Why, there's scarcely a gunshot to be heard on a Saturday night nowadays."

Calvin heaved a sigh and turned to leave, but Mr. Sullivan wasn't finished.

"What we got here now is civilization," he hollered after us. "It's spreading faster than smallpox. Pretty soon the whole West is going to be like Dodge City."

"More's the pity," Calvin muttered.

Dragging Caesar along with the help of a rope tied round his neck, I followed Calvin down a dusty side street, past deserted saloons and dance halls. There were burned-out places too, nothing left but charred timbers and ashes. No one seemed interested in giving anything to a poor orphan child and his consumptive brother. Even Caesar's most pitiful performance went unappreciated.

Although we didn't make a cent in Dodge, Calvin managed to lose more than half of our money to a pickpocket even more skillful than he was. It was lucky he'd had the foresight to put thirty dollars in his boot, or we'd have lost it all.

After eating a tough steak, more gristle than meat, we ended up in the Grand Imperial Hotel down by the railroad depot. A sign in the lobby said NO MORE THAN FIVE TO A BED, but fortunately for me, the crowds were long gone. The clerk gave us a room the size of an outhouse, but at least it had two beds and enough room for Caesar to curl up in a corner. The sheets looked like they hadn't been changed in recent history, and soon after I lay down, little varmints commenced biting me.

I swear I would have slept better rolled up in my blankets on the hard ground, but I didn't complain. My wish had at long last been granted—the next day Calvin and I would be boarding the morning train to Colorado. After whispering good night to Caesar, I fell fast asleep, bedbugs and all.

10

A T THE TRAIN DEPOT, CALVIN TRIED TO persuade the ticket agent to let us ride free, but his sweet talk about us being poor orphans got him nowhere. The man had obviously heard every type of hard-luck story the mind can devise. We had to settle for a third-class carriage to Pueblo, Colorado, which was as far as we could go without spending all our money.

When the train came in two hours late, I rushed ahead of Calvin, dragging Caesar behind me, pushing and shoving through the crowd. It seemed everybody in town was aiming to wedge themselves into the passenger cars. In my haste, I almost knocked a lady down, earning a whack from her parasol that brought tears to my eyes.

Calvin and Caesar and I ended up in a car that resembled a long, narrow wooden box with an aisle down the middle and rows of hard seats on either side. We squeezed ourselves into a place hardly big enough for anyone but a baby or very small child. Somehow I persuaded Caesar to lie down and stay out of sight.

Once we got settled, I thought we'd leave right away, but I swear we sat there sweltering for over an hour while they unloaded the baggage car and then reloaded it. Lord, the flies were something awful. A baby right behind me was screaming in my ear, and the man in front of me must have eaten too many beans for lunch. Between him, the cigar smoke, and the stink coming from the convenience room at the end of the car, I thought I'd never get out of Kansas with my nose intact.

When I started fussing, Calvin said, "If Roscoe hadn't stolen my money, we'd be traveling in a first-class Pullman car, sitting on soft velvet seats in the company of refined persons of quality."

He sounded right testy. Unlike me, the Gentleman Outlaw wasn't used to living like somebody's poor relation. I took the hint, though, and stopped complaining.

Around three o'clock, the train gave a tremendous lurch. The whistle blew and we were off. I was hoping a good cool wind would blow all the bad smells away, but instead, cinders and smoke blew inside and added to my discomfort. So far, train travel was not as grand as I'd expected.

The car got hotter and stuffier. The wheels went

clickety clickety click, clickety clickety clack. We rocked back and forth, back and forth, like babies in a cradle. All round me, droning voices mimicked a chorus of insects on an August afternoon. My head bobbed up and down, and my eyelids sunk like they were weighted with lead sinkers.

I slept and woke, slept and woke. *Clickety clickety click, clickety clickety clack.* On we rode into a sunset as red as fire and just as hot. Stopping here, stopping there. Folks getting off, folks getting on. Babies crying, children fussing, men cursing, women whispering.

When it got dark, the conductor lit oil lamps that looked like they might come crashing down and set the car afire. A boy passed through selling things from a box—soap and towels, bed boards and pillows stuffed with straw, coffee, water, canned food and dried food. At the sight of it, my stomach lurched with hunger, but Calvin said we couldn't afford the prices the little cheat was asking.

Finally I fell into a deep sleep from which I woke at dawn. At long last, we were in Colorado. Sticking my head out the window, I got my first look at the Rockies way off in the distance, snow-topped against the blue sky. Coming from Kansas, I'd never seen their like before and could scarcely wait to get nearer and see how tall the mountains really were.

When we pulled into Pueblo, Calvin gave me a nudge. "Get moving, Eli," he said. "We don't want to go on to Denver."

With Caesar leading, I shoved my way off the train. Oh, but it felt good to stand on solid ground again.

"I'm so hungry," I said, eyeing the depot restaurant everyone was rushing into. "Can we afford a cup of coffee and a roll?"

"Wait till the people who are getting back on the train finish eating," Calvin said. "You'll be trampled to death if you go in there now."

It's good I took his advice, because you never saw such a combobulous commotion. Those passengers had twenty minutes to eat, and they were hollering orders and grabbing tables and stuffing food down their throats like someone was going to steal it if they didn't swallow it fast. I swear I saw a man grab a sandwich right out of a little tyke's hand and run out the door with it before anybody could catch him.

When the engineer blasted the whistle, the passengers came dashing out of the restaurant, choking down food as they ran, and piled into the cars. In no time at all, the train was under way, huffing and puffing north to Denver, showering Calvin, Caesar, and me with cinders.

When we ventured into the restaurant, we saw chairs on the floor, overturned tables, spilled food and drink everywhere. Cinders gritted under our feet; they covered the windowsills; they peppered the food, pies, and cakes as well as everything else, including my clothes and hair.

We picked the cleanest table we could find, and Caesar crept underneath as if he sensed it was the safest place.

When the waitress brought our food, half my coffee had slopped into my saucer. The rolls were hard as stone, but I found soaking them in the coffee softened them up. Made the coffee taste a mite better too.

While we ate, Calvin told me he'd come up with a new moneymaking scheme. Three-card monte, he called it. A surefire way to get rich fast.

"I don't know what you're talking about," I said, too weary to put up with high-flown words and silly notions.

Without another word, Calvin pulled a brand-new pack of playing cards out of his pocket. Where or when he'd gotten them I hadn't the slightest idea, but I was too fascinated by his skill to ask any questions. Instead, I watched him fan out the two of spades, the jack of diamonds, and the ace of hearts. Turning them face down, he shuffled the three cards and spread them out on the table. Lordy, but he was fast.

"To win, all you have to do is pick the ace," he said, his eyes as mischievous as a crow's when it's about to play a trick.

I studied the backs of the cards so long Calvin lost patience. "We haven't got all day, Eli. For the Lord's sake, take one. They won't bite."

I shut my eyes and grabbed. My card turned out to be the jack.

Calvin smiled and scooped up the cards. He shuffled them and laid them back down. "Go ahead, Eli. Try again."

This time I came up with the two of spades. Once more Calvin shuffled and I picked. I tried over and over again, but no matter how close I watched him shuffle those cards, I never once picked the ace of hearts. After seven tries, I gave up.

"You're just too good," I muttered. "I can't beat you."

Calvin smiled and sat back. "That's correct, Eli. You can't beat me. No one can. Let me demonstrate."

Shuffling slowly, he showed me how he used those quick fingers of his to substitute a second jack of diamonds for the ace of hearts. By the time he told me to pick a card, he'd tucked the ace up his sleeve. No wonder I never won.

"Where did you learn such a dirty way of cheating?" I asked him.

Calvin frowned as if he didn't care for my choice of words. "It's a game my father taught me."

"Why, you told me your daddy was a man among men, the best cardplayer ever, better even than Doc Holliday," I said, too disgusted to watch my tongue. "It appears to me Mr. Calvin Thaddeus Featherbone, Senior, was nothing but a common low-down card-sharp. No wonder he got himself shot!"

Calvin's face flushed. For a moment I thought he was going to explode like a stick of dynamite, but instead he took a deep breath and said, "Confound it, Eli, don't climb on that high horse of yours. I need you to play a small part in the game."

I shoved my chair back and got to my feet. "Oh no, not me," I said. "I don't aim to get myself shot by some old coot like Roscoe Suggs."

Calvin leaped up and caught me. "Listen here, Elijah Bates. People who gamble are greedy fools. They don't deserve your sympathy."

Keeping hold of me, he dragged me outside. In a kindlier voice, he said, "We'll make money fast playing three-card monte. That means we'll arrive in Tinville sooner."

I quit struggling then and let Calvin lead me down the street. Much as I disliked the idea of cheating, I wanted to get to Tinville as quickly as possible. And that rascal knew it.

"All you have to do is stand in the back of the crowd and watch," Calvin said as sweet as honey. "After three or four players lose, people are bound to accuse me of cheating. When they do, push your way to the front and ask to play. I'll say no, you're too young, but you insist. Eventually I'll give up and take your money."

He paused and grinned at me. "I'll make sure you pick the ace of hearts, Eli. When the crowd sees you win, they'll clamor to play."

Without returning Calvin's jaw-stretching grin, I nodded glumly and trudged along beside him. As far as schemes go, I suppose it could have been worse. At least it didn't sound like I'd get shot.

11

CALVIN'S NEW SCHEME STARTED OUT FAIRLY well. He found an old wooden box, set it on end near one of the busier saloons, and positioned himself behind it. He'd washed up on the train and slicked his hair back and dusted off his shirt and trousers as well as he could, but any fool could tell he was down on his luck. I supposed his looks might help. Who would expect a young man as pale and handsome as curly-headed Calvin Featherbone to be a cheating, lying rascal?

While Caesar and I hung around in the background, trying to look inconspicuous, Calvin drew a crowd with a spiel that went like this. Holding up three cards, he fanned them this way and that to attract attention.

"Gentlemen," he called out, "you see before you a poor young man desperately in need of money. I hold my heart in my hand, sirs." With that, he waved the ace of hearts. "Take a chance and see if you can draw my heart from a pile of three. Keep close watch now."

Throwing the cards face down, Calvin shuffled them with those agile fingers of his. "Here's the heart," he cried, slipping it in and out of the cards so fast my eyes were dazzled. "Now here. Now there. Now where?"

He paused and smiled at the growing mob of bearded miners, Chinese railroad workers, and travelers between trains like us. I expected one of them to holler, "It's up your sleeve, you lying little cheat," but no one said a word.

"You win if you take my heart," Calvin went on in a softer voice. "I win if I keep my heart. Your chances are one in three, gentlemen. Mine are two in three, which gives me the edge, I admit."

Flourishing the ace of hearts, he surveyed the crowd. "All you need to beat the odds are sharp eyes, gentlemen. Come, who'll give me five dollars to steal my heart away?"

After some hesitancy, a scruffy miner stepped forward and slapped a five-dollar gold coin on the box top. "I reckon I can affort to part with that and a whole lot more if I have to."

I held my breath when the miner lost, but instead of accusing Calvin of cheating, the fool went and slapped down another coin. After four tries, he gave up and headed toward the saloon.

A tall gent with the look of a salesman said the miner was blind in one eye and couldn't see out of the other. He insisted on laying down twenty dollars, thinking he'd win the miner's losses as well as Calvin's. Naturally he lost too.

This went on for quite a while. After Calvin had won more money than I'd seen in my whole entire life, some folks started grumbling.

"It's mighty peculiar nobody wins but you, sir," the salesman said. Unlike the other losers, he'd hung around, watching one man after another empty his pockets on Calvin's box top.

This was my cue. With Caesar at my heels, I pushed my way timidly to the front of the crowd, apologizing for every foot I stepped on, minding my manners just as Calvin had instructed me to. He'd convinced me a body could get away with almost anything, including highway robbery, as long as he said "please" and "thank you."

When he saw me approach the box, Calvin frowned and shook his head. "I don't accept money from children," he said.

"But you're scarcely more than a child yourself, sir," I piped up. "Surely you must take pity on such as me and let me try my luck."

I put a silver dollar on the box. "It ain't much, but it's all I got, sir. You know it won't last me long, so what does it matter if I lose it now or later?"

A ripple of sympathy ran through the crowd,

especially from the ladies, who weren't gambling themselves but enjoying the spectacle of seeing rogues and rascals lose to a handsome young man like Calvin.

Calvin shook his head. "How could I sleep tonight knowing I'd taken your last dollar? Go to church, boy, as I should have done when I was your age. Pray to the Lord to help you. Don't fall into evil ways as I have."

At this, Caesar whined and nudged me with his nose as if he too was aiming to save my soul.

The murmuring grew a little louder. One lady said, "Let the child play. If he loses, I'll give him a dollar myself."

Before Calvin could accept her offer, a tall, thin gentleman stepped up to the box and laid down a ten-dollar gold piece. "I'll play for the boy," he said. "If I win, he can keep the money free and clear." He returned the silver dollar to my pocket, and the crowd clapped and whistled.

Calvin glanced at me, his face pale. He'd clipped the corner of the ace of hearts so I'd be sure to find it. If he put that card on the table, the stranger was bound to notice. It was clear Calvin would have to go on cheating. Either way, he was taking a risk, I thought, as the gentleman had a sharp-eyed, hollow-cheeked look that reminded me of a half-starved wolf.

"Well?" The gentleman eyed Calvin impatiently.

Or was it suspiciously? "Do you accept my offer or not?"

From the corner of my eye, I made a further study of the gentleman's appearance. He wore a fancy black coat over a white shirt, a black tie knotted loose around his neck. In its folds glittered a stone that might have been glass but more likely was a genuine diamond. On his head was a slouch hat. Its brim hid most of his face but not his fancy handlebar mustache, waxed to perfection, or his long brown hair.

A revolver hung on one hip for all to see. I didn't doubt for a moment he knew how to use it.

In short, the fellow was the very image of what Calvin himself wanted to be—handsome, well dressed, and dangerous. If he were to step off the train in Tinville, someone would run for the sheriff straightaway.

I felt as edgy as a dog in a thunderstorm, but if Calvin was rattled, he didn't show it. Without hesitating, he went into his routine of fast shuffling.

The gentleman's sharp eyes followed every move those hands made, but Calvin kept his patter going and then stood back to let the gentleman try his luck.

The gentleman studied the cards intently. Sunlight sparkled on the golden eagle he'd laid on the box. It was so quiet I thought I heard the fleas on Caesar's back hopping from one spot to another.

Finally the gentleman leaned over the crate and

picked a card. Quick as a wink, he held up the ace of hearts. Everyone in the audience gave a huge sigh of relief to see my good fortune.

Except me. I knew full well there was no ace among those three cards. It was up Calvin's sleeve. When the gentleman leaned over the crate, he must have slipped an ace out of his own sleeve.

It seemed Calvin had met his equal in tricks, maybe even his better. From the look on his face, the Gentleman Outlaw was no doubt thinking the same thing.

Taking a matching gold piece from Calvin, the gentleman turned to me with a smile and handed me the two coins. "Put these someplace safe," he said, eyeing Calvin. "The money's yours and yours alone, boy."

"Thank you, sir." I dropped the gold eagles into my overalls pocket, gazing into the gentleman's dark eyes all the while. It was a little like matching stares with a deadly snake.

Although I expected him to denounce Calvin as a fraud, he didn't utter a word. He simply stood there watching the Gentleman Outlaw begin his spiel again. Calvin's forehead was beaded with perspiration, but his fingers were as quick as ever and his voice didn't shake.

I admired his nerve. Doc Holliday himself couldn't have been more composed under pressure than Calvin Featherbone.

After a while, I remembered I was supposed to lie low till it was time to board the train late at night. If folks saw me with Calvin, they'd guess I was his accomplice. There was no telling what kind of ruckus that might cause.

I looked back once. The tall gentleman was still watching Calvin. I don't think either he or Calvin noticed my departure.

Using my silver dollar, I bought supper for Caesar and me and went over to the depot to wait for Calvin. A pretty little crescent moon smiled down at me from the starry sky, but the night air was cold. I was grateful to have Caesar beside me, big and warm.

To pass the time, I pulled my harmonica out of my pocket and began playing. Just for myself, not for money, enjoying the happy sounds I was making. No sad tunes tonight. We were rich, Calvin and me. Tomorrow we'd be on our way to Tinville.

All of a sudden, a tall figure in black stepped out of the shadows and sat on the baggage cart beside me. It was the mysterious gentleman, my benefactor. He'd moved so silently I hadn't even heard his footsteps.

"You play very well," he said in a voice honeyed by years in Dixie. "Tell me, do you know 'Shenandoah'?"

"Sure." I played the song nice and slow, bringing out all its sadness, and he sat beside me, smoking one of those long, skinny cigars, a melancholy expression softening his bony features.

When I was done, he thanked me and asked if I still had the two gold eagles he'd given me.

I touched my pocket to feel their outline under the cloth. "'Course I do."

"I'm glad to hear it, boy," said he. "Because that's just about all you've got in this world."

I stared at him, thinking of the hundreds of dollars Calvin had collected from the townsfolk. I realized too that he knew there was a connection between Calvin and me. My mouth dried up and my heart beat faster. "What do you mean?" I asked, trying to keep my voice from shaking. "Where's Calvin? Has he been robbed?"

"The fool lost every cent at the faro table," the gentleman said. "I warned him the game was as rigged as three-card monte, but he insisted he could outsharp the dealer. Serves him right, I suppose."

I couldn't take in the man's words. "But Calvin's the best card player alive today," I stammered. "His daddy taught him everything he knew, and he was even better than Doc Holliday himself."

"Was he indeed?" The man's laughter turned to a cough. When he recovered, he reached into his pocket and gave me two more gold eagles. "If you plan to go on shilling for a tinhorn gambler, you'll need this, my boy."

My face turned so red it's a wonder it didn't light the night like a candle. "How the Sam Hill did you know Calvin and I were working together?"

The man laughed again. "I'd be a daisy if I failed to notice something so painfully obvious." He leaned closer and tapped my knee. "To tell the truth, your friend was fortunate he attracted a crowd of ignoramuses today. Three-card monte is a beginner's game, boy, a beginner's game. Tell Calvin not to try it in the streets of Durango or Silverton. He'll be run out of town on a rail."

Getting to his feet, the man gave Caesar a pat on the head. "My train's arriving," he said. "Farewell, young fellow. And good luck to you."

Touching the brim of his hat, my mysterious benefactor strode down the platform and vanished in the cloud of steam billowing out from under an incoming locomotive.

"Thank you, sir, thank you," I called, half tempted to follow him onto the train and beg him to take me to Tinville. He seemed worthier of my trust and gratitude than Calvin Featherbone.

But the gentleman didn't look back. Nor did I have the nerve to chase after him like a lost puppy.

Long after the train left, I sat on the baggage cart, fingering the four gold coins and thinking. Surely Calvin hadn't gambled away our fortune. It made my stomach churn to think of it. If the money was gone, how would we ever get to Tinville?

Gazing into Caesar's big brown eyes, I showed him the gold coins. "I've got forty dollars, boy. Do you think we should leave Calvin and go off on our own?"

Caesar whined and licked my nose.

"Is that a yes or a no?" I asked.

Caesar curled up beside me, sighed, and closed his eyes. When he started snoring, I figured he was advising me to stay. And, to tell you the truth, that's what I was inclined to do. If nothing else, I wanted a chance to tell Mr. Calvin Thaddeus Featherbone, the Second, exactly what I thought of him and his no-good, low-down ways.

12

ALONG ABOUT 2 A.M., CALVIN WOKE ME UP.
I'd fallen asleep on the baggage cart and was so
stiff I could barely move, but I had little time to
think of my own discomfort. To my extreme shock
and utter disgust, the so-called Gentleman Outlaw
was drunk to the point he could scarcely talk.

What he did say I wished I hadn't heard. Every
word the mysterious gentleman had spoken was
true. Calvin had gambled most of our money away
and then spent the rest on whiskey.

"The dealer cheated," Calvin claimed. "I saw him,
and when I spoke up he threatened to shoot me. All
that saved me was not having a gun. The scoundrel
said he'd never fired at an unarmed man and didn't
intend to begin with a greenhorn like me."

Calvin spit in the dust and nearly fell on his face.
"The very idea," he mumbled, "calling me a greenhorn! If I'd had my Colt, I'd have put a bullet

between his eyes, which were so crossed I don't know how he could see straight."

Taking Caesar with me, I slid off the baggage cart and put some distance between Calvin and me. He reeked of whiskey and cigars and all sorts of sinful nastiness. If this was what men came to, maybe being a girl wasn't as bad as I thought.

"If you expect me to take pity on you, you're in for a mighty big surprise," I hollered, thinking if I yelled loud enough I wouldn't cry, which would be a very girlish thing to do. "That was our train fare, you low-down skunk! Now how are we going to get to Tinville?"

To my surprise, Calvin commenced to apologize, making promises so foolish nobody with a grain of sense would believe them. Suddenly he seemed downright pathetic, all dirty and rumpled and still acting like a fine gentleman, using big words when little ones would have done just as well if not better. Though I struggled against it, I felt my heart go as soft as a rotten apple.

"How far will twenty dollars get us?" I asked, keeping my voice as tough and hard as Little Homer's. Calvin knew I had those two gold pieces, so it made no sense to hold them back. But the other twenty dollars were my secret. Calvin had no way of knowing the mysterious gentleman had taken pity on me twice. And he wasn't going to find out.

Calvin walked over to the ticket window and squinted at the fare table. "It appears we have enough to get to Alamosa," he said. "We'll earn some money there and then go on."

By the time the ticket agent showed up, Calvin had doused his head in a horse trough and sobered up a bit. I handed over two of my eagles, but I kept the other two in my left shoe where I hoped they'd be safe.

→>•◄←

We rode third class again, which meant seats about as comfortable as church pews, but since it was now 4 A.M., the three of us fell sound asleep in no time.

When I woke up, the sun was shining in my eyes. It was a little after six and we were pulling into Cuchara Junction. The mountains were much closer. Bigger too. After seeing the flat land of Kansas all my life, I noticed the sky seemed smaller here. You couldn't see forever the way you could back home.

"Those are the Sangre de Cristo Mountains," said Calvin, sounding more like his regular old smarty-pants self. "It's Spanish for *Blood of Christ*."

The train jerked to a stop and the conductor yelled, "All out for breakfast. Train leaves in twenty minutes, so make it snappy, folks."

I shoved Calvin. "If you want to eat, get moving."

He gave me a bleary-eyed look and shook his head. "No thanks, Elijah. I can't stomach the food I'd be likely to get in that hellhole."

"Well, mind Caesar then. I'm half starved."

Somehow I managed to grab a table and get coffee and rolls from a waitress even sloppier than the one we'd met in Pueblo. I wolfed it down and ran back to the train without a minute to spare.

After we left Cuchara, the train climbed higher and higher into the mountains. *Sangre de Cristo.* I rolled the words around in my mouth, savoring their foreign taste. It was a peculiar name, but maybe it meant those old Spanish explorers suffered a lot looking for the cities of gold they never found.

We made a short stop in a little town called La Veta to unload freight and take on a few passengers. Then we went on up the mountain. On one side of the train was a rocky wall. On the other, the ground dropped way down so all you saw out the window were sky and more mountains in the distance. For once I didn't stick my head out to get a better view. Frankly, I didn't want to know how far up we were.

Sometime after eleven, we arrived in Alamosa, another dusty town abustle with the usual mix of folks—railroad workers, miners, cowboys, gamblers, Spaniards, and Indians. Some were heading south to Espanola in the New Mexico Territory, and others were heading west toward Durango and Silverton to try their luck at the silver camps.

"So what do you intend to do now, Calvin?" I asked. "Thanks to you, we're dead broke." It was a mean thing to say, but I wanted to see him wince.

Calvin was busy wiping his boot on the side of a horse trough. When he'd scraped it clean, he turned to me. "We're not quite broke, Eli."

With a smile, he reached toward me and pretended to pull two gold eagles out of my ear. "My, my, where did these come from?"

Too late, I grabbed at the coins. The rotten pickpocketing son of a gun must have stolen them while I was dozing on the train.

"Give them back, you thief!" I shouted. "They're mine!"

"Yours?" Calvin eyed me. The coins jingled in his pocket. "And from whom did you steal them, Eli?"

"The gentleman who outsmarted you at three-card monte gave them to me! Me—not you!"

Calvin's eyes widened in surprise. "That scoundrel? Why, he's the very one who took me to the gambling house where I lost my money. It's my belief he and the faro dealer were a pair of swindlers. That rogue wouldn't give a penny to his own mother, let alone some scalawag like you."

"All's I know is he found me down at the depot and told me you'd lost all our money at the faro table. Claimed he warned you the game was rigged but you wouldn't listen. Oh no, not you who knows everything and thinks he's better at cards than Doc Holliday himself!"

I was hopping mad, but my temper just made Calvin laugh. To shut him up, I kicked his shins with my old clodhoppers. A woman passing by gave a little gasp.

Calvin winced. "You wretched little urchin," he muttered. "I ought to give you a good whipping for that."

I put up my fists just as Little Homer did when he got into one of his many scrapes. "Go ahead, try it. I'm ready for you, I'll give as good as I get!"

Calvin backed off then and tried to calm me down. "Listen, Elijah," he said when I was breathing normally again. "This money will finance the scheme I've been perfecting."

"Oh, tarnation," I muttered. "What lunatic idea has lodged in your brain now?"

Calvin smiled. There was something in his eyes I didn't especially trust.

"Why are you looking at me like that?" I asked, edging away as I spoke.

"You're the dirtiest boy I've ever seen," Calvin replied. "I don't believe you've taken a bath in all the time we've been together."

"Well, how the dickens am I supposed to wash?" It seemed to me this conversation was headed in a bad direction. Finding privacy for my natural body functions was hard enough without figuring out ways to bathe so Calvin wouldn't see anything he shouldn't see.

We happened to be standing in front of a sorry old hotel that advertised baths for a penny. Soap and towels two cents extra.

Calvin pointed to the sign. "Since it's essential for us to look respectable, I'm going to see you get a good scrubbing."

I started running, but Calvin was too fast for me. Quick as a rattlesnake, his hand flew out and grabbed my overalls straps. He hauled me back so fast my feet lifted clear off the ground.

"Sic him, Caesar," I yelled at my dog. "Bite the miserable son of a gun's leg off!"

Unfortunately, Calvin had worked his charm on Caesar long ago. Pretending it was all a game, the mangy mutt frolicked about, grinning and wagging his tail and trying to lick my face as well as Calvin's.

Calvin dragged me wiggling and shouting into the hotel parlor. Caesar circled us, still wagging his tail and barking good-naturedly.

The Royal Hotel was the dirtiest, most wretched place I ever saw in my life. Mean-eyed men were lounging around, chewing tobacco and spitting on the floor, though there was a perfectly good spittoon within easy reach. Maybe they were scared of soiling it. They all stared at Calvin, Caesar, and me as if they'd never seen our like before—and most probably they hadn't, as I was still screeching and hollering and flailing about. The desk clerk scowled and demanded to know what Calvin was up to.

"This filthy child and I are here for a bath," Calvin said, making an effort to be heard over my howls.

"No!" I screamed, still kicking. "No!"

Without intending to, the desk clerk saved my hide by telling Calvin he only allowed one bather per tub. "If you both wish to wash—which I highly recommend—you'll have to pay for the use of two tubs."

It was just an excuse to gouge money out of dirty travelers, and Calvin knew it, but for some reason that bath was so important to him he coughed up six cents with only a faint mumble of complaint.

"As for the dog—" the clerk began but then just sort of ran out of words.

"Don't worry about Caesar," I said. "He's never had a bath in his life and he doesn't plan to start now."

The clerk sniffed and made a face, but I imagine he'd smelled a lot worse than Caesar, working in a dump like this.

Turning away, he called a woman to fetch hot water, towels, and soap.

In the washroom were a couple of hip tubs separated by a sheet hung on a rope. Not much privacy—especially if a person has a reason to hide his or her body. What saved me was the hot water. The woman brought a cauldron from the stove. When she poured it in the tub, the steam rose up dense enough for me to strip fast and jump in before Calvin saw anything—which meant I just about cooked myself.

I scrubbed till I was as pink as an Easter ham. If I missed a spot, Calvin might decide to wash me himself. I could hear him on the other side of the sheet, splashing around and singing "O, Susanna!" It seemed to me he'd recovered his spirits mighty fast.

After a few minutes he called out, "Are you clean, Eli?"

"Yes!" I hollered, but he came to check anyway. Thank the Lord, he'd put on his trousers. I sunk down in the water, glad my chest was still as bony and flat as a boy's. As for the rest of me, I prayed the soapsuds were thick enough to keep him from noticing anything strange about my lower regions.

"Whew," said Calvin. "Just look at that water. It's positively black. I hope that's proof you've scrubbed the dirt off."

All of a sudden he reached out and grabbed my locket. "What the dickens is this?"

I tried to pull away, but I was afraid of breaking the little silver chain. Besides he already had it open and was studying Mama's and Papa's tiny faces.

"This is a peculiar thing for a boy to wear around his neck," Calvin said.

I huddled in the dirty water, so scared I could hardly breathe. "That's Mama and Papa," I whispered. "I wear it so's I won't forget them."

Like Miss Pearl, Calvin nodded sympathetically and snapped the locket shut. Letting go of the chain, he watched it fall back against my chest. "Do you intend to soak in that dirty water all day?"

"You go away," I muttered. "Then I'll get out."

Calvin laughed. "If you aren't the biggest Nancy-boy I ever saw. Do you think I care what in Sam Hill you look like naked?"

When he reached for my arm, I slid under the water, praying I was too slippery for him to get a good grip on me.

"Lord, Eli, if it bothers you so much, I'll turn my back. I don't want to be responsible for a drowning."

When I was sure he'd done as he promised, I scrambled out of the tub and pulled on my clothes without even bothering to dry myself first. I couldn't help noticing how nasty my shirt and overalls felt against my clean skin. They were so dirty they could have stood up all by themselves.

"Are you decent yet?" Calvin asked.

For an answer, I wanted to kick him in the rear end, but I didn't dare. I just said, "Yes," and stood there red-faced while he inspected me.

"Except for the lamentable condition of your clothing, you look almost respectable," he said. "Not perfect, mind you, but definitely an improvement."

Taking a deep breath, I followed Calvin and Caesar outside, still feeling shaky. First the bath, then the locket. I'd come perilously close to giving away my most precious secrets. If my true name and nature were gold coins, the Gentleman Outlaw would surely have pulled them out of my ears by now.

13

OUR FIRST STOP WAS A GENTLEMEN'S CLOTH-
ing store. After tying Caesar to a hitching post
by the door, Calvin led me inside.

"Good afternoon, sir," he said to the clerk, just as
polite as can be. "My brother and I need to be outfitted with a decent set of clothes, as you can plainly
see."

The clerk nodded. He could indeed plainly see.
And smell, too. Wrinkling his nose in annoyance,
he said, "If you're seeking to buy overalls, try the
general store on Front Street."

Calvin gave the man a stare cold enough to
freeze his eyeballs and slapped my gold eagles down
on the counter. "I don't wish to repeat myself," he
said softly. "I want a suit for the boy and one for
myself, as well as shirts, ties, good shoes, stockings,
and proper underwear. All of the finest quality. Do
you understand?"

The clerk began to perspire. "Certainly, sir, certainly," he murmured. "I'll begin with your brother. A fine lad, sir, a fine lad indeed."

For reasons of my own, I was even more nervous than the clerk. My raggedy overalls and shirt were all that shielded me from the world. If I had to strip, I'd have a heap of explaining to do.

Calvin must have sensed what was bothering me because he said, "Eli's as shy as a girl. I doubt he's wearing proper underwear, so give him a set to put on before you start measuring and fitting him for a suit."

In the privacy of a closet under the stairs, I managed to button myself up decent in a suit of boy's underwear, but I felt mighty peculiar walking around the store in such skimpy apparel. Neither Calvin nor the clerk noticed anything amiss—which proves, I reckon, that folks see what they expect to see. Dress like a boy, walk like a boy, call yourself by a boy's name, and everybody will believe you are indeed a boy.

I stood real still and let the clerk go about his business with a measuring tape. Under Calvin's watchful eye, he outfitted me in a black Eton jacket and matching knee-length trousers, a white shirt with a stiff stand-up collar, a neck tie tight enough to choke a pig, scratchy black wool stockings, and shiny black shoes that pinched my toes. By the time he was done with me, I hardly recognized myself. I looked for all the world like the sort of pitiful panty-waist Little Homer would delight in tormenting.

"You're a dandy now," Calvin said, placing a black yacht cap on my head. "I wager your own father wouldn't know you."

I would have laughed up the sleeve of my new jacket if I hadn't been so worried about the cost of it. My suit was over three dollars, my shirt was sixty-five cents, my cap a quarter, underwear half a dollar, hose a quarter, and shoes a dollar sixty, for a grand total of almost seven dollars. I had never thought I'd see the day anyone would spend that much money on me.

As for Calvin, his outfit brought the cost to seventeen dollars and twenty cents. I swallowed hard when the clerk dropped my precious gold coins into the till and handed Calvin two dollars and eighty cents change. We left our old clothes for the clerk to throw away. They weren't good for anything else.

Outside the shop, Calvin lounged against the rail while I untied Caesar. I was scared the poor dog might not recognize me, but he wagged his tail and licked my hands as if he were complimenting me on my new appearance.

Finally I turned to Calvin. "What are we going to do now?" I asked, not even trying to control the fear that pitched my voice high as a girl's. "All we have is two dollars and eighty cents. Where are we going to sleep tonight? How are we getting to Tinville?"

Instead of answering my questions, Calvin gestured at the crowded boardwalks. "Take a good look at the men of this town, Eli."

"I see them," I grumbled, surveying the scene. Miners led donkeys laden with saddlebags. Drunken louts roamed from gambling hall to saloon and back again. They cursed and yelled and shoved each other. Every now and then some fool would shoot a gun into the air and holler. I'd seen their kind in almost every town we'd passed through.

"A fine bunch they are," I said. "Ignorant fools and loud-mouthed braggarts. And you no better than the worst of them."

"Right in your assessment of them," Calvin said, "but wrong in your assessment of me." Laying a hand on my shoulder, he grinned like a hungry fox. "What you see, Eli, is a passel of jackasses begging to lose a year's earnings in a couple of hours at the gambling tables."

"And you're just the one to help them do it," I muttered, kicking at a clod of dried-up horse dung.

Calvin tipped his expensive new hat and gave me a smile no one could resist, man, woman, or child. "Come along, Eli. Hold your head up, show off your new finery, attract attention."

Tipping his hat to ladies and gents alike, Calvin moseyed along the wooden sidewalk. In spite of myself, I began to enjoy the way folks looked at us. I'd never gotten a second glance from anybody before. Not as a girl in faded, outgrown dresses nor as a boy in raggedy overalls. But in my new duds, I cut a fine figure. People turned their heads and stared at me as well as Calvin.

Even Caesar held his head up. If another dog looked his way, he ignored him. Today he was just too good to squabble with ordinary old town dogs.

After a stop at the barber shop for twenty-five-cent haircuts and a dash of good-smelling tonic, Calvin and I rented a cheap room at the Broadwell Hotel. The walls were thin, and noise from the saloon downstairs came up through the floor, but Calvin said we'd soon be in a position to afford better.

Caesar made himself comfortable in the middle of one of the beds. He wasn't supposed to be in the room, but the way things were, I figured he had no more fleas than the miners. In fact, the poor dog was probably in greater danger of catching something from them than the other way around. Anyways, we had the best old time bouncing on the bed till grumpy Calvin hollered at us to behave ourselves.

"We're supposed to be grieving the loss of our dear mother and father, who departed this vale of tears one month ago."

I stared at Calvin, puzzled by his words. "Where did they go?"

He sighed. "They *died,* Eli."

"Well, tarnation, why didn't you say so instead of going on about veils of tears and such?"

"An educated person avoids offending the delicate ears of others with such bald, unadorned truths."

I poked Caesar. "Listen to the gentleman, sir. He's attempting to fancify us."

Caesar rolled over on his back, paws in the air, and played dead.

Calvin wasn't amused by Caesar's antics. "Please make an effort to be serious, Elijah," he said in that soft rattlesnake hiss he used when he was riled about something.

Sitting me down on the bed, he explained his latest scheme. We were greenhorns from back east, he said, grieving the loss of our parents but planning to make a new start in Colorado. In the saloon, Calvin would have a couple of whiskeys and pretend to be drunk. The miners would think him an easy mark and invite him to join a card game.

"I'll lose for a while," Calvin said. "You'll beg me to stop, but I'll go on playing. The stakes will rise. When I'm down to my last silver dollar, my luck will suddenly change."

I stared at Calvin, thinking he'd gone plumb stark raving mad. "And just what are you planning to gamble with? I doubt the miners are generous enough to let you play for free."

Calvin smiled. "Leave that to me, Eli."

When he headed for the door, I jumped to my feet. "Where are you going? What are you aiming to do?"

"Let's just say I'm going to see a man about a

dog." Calvin paused and looked at me. "You stay here, Eli, and try to stay out of trouble."

I watched him run down the steps to the hotel lobby, my head awhirl with speculations. Was he planning to rob a bank, pick people's pockets, hold up a stagecoach? Had he bought a gun when I wasn't looking? Or, more likely, stolen one?

And why in tarnation did he want another dog? Wasn't Caesar enough?

Unable to stand it another second, I ran down the stairs after Calvin, but by the time I got to the street, Caesar at my heels, there was no sign of him. I pushed through the crowds, ducking and shoving, looking in saloons and gambling halls, but even with Caesar's nose to help sniff him out, the Gentleman Outlaw had just plain vanished.

Finally I gave up and trudged back to the hotel. For a while, I played my harmonica and made Caesar practice his tricks. When I grew tired of that, I lay on my bed and watched the shadows change on the walls as the sun sank lower and lower.

Every now and then I'd get up and look out the window, hoping to catch a glimpse of Calvin's curly head, but he was never among the crowd traipsing the streets.

The later it got, the more I worried. Where in tarnation was he? Why didn't he come back? What if something bad had happened to him?

Just as I was about to give him up for dead, Calvin

strode into the room, looking as jaunty as a million-aire.

"Where have you been?" I asked him. "I've been worried sick!"

Calvin shrugged and brushed a speck of dust off his sleeve. "I told you. I went to see a man about a dog."

"Well, where is it?"

"Where is what?"

"The dog."

Calvin stared at me. "Dog?"

"The one you went to see the man about," I said, trying my best to be patient. "Did you tie him up outside or something?"

Calvin sighed as if realizing he hadn't yet plumbed the full depth of my ignorance. "That is an expression one uses when one does not wish to reveal the true nature of one's business," he said in the snootiest voice he'd come up with yet.

I flopped down on my bed and scowled at Calvin. Here I'd been thinking Caesar was about to have his own friend and traveling companion. I was glad I hadn't mentioned it to him. The poor dog might have gotten his hopes up.

"Well, just what the Sam Hill were you doing all this time?" I asked.

Calvin reached into his pocket and pulled out a leather pouch. With a grand flourish, he emptied it on the bed. Silver dollars rolled off in all directions, clinking and jingling like sleigh bells. The two of us gathered them up, and Calvin stacked them neatly on the dresser.

"One hundred dollars," I whispered. "Wherever did you get it?"

"Perhaps I pulled it out of people's ears," Calvin said, pretending to find more coins in my ears.

I jerked away, irked by his teasing. There was only one way Calvin could have gotten that much money. He'd gone and robbed a bank without taking me along. I didn't know whether to be mad at missing the experience or glad I hadn't seen Calvin risking his life.

"You didn't shoot anybody, did you?" I whispered. Lord, I wasn't about to touch money tainted with some poor man's innocent blood.

Calvin shook his head. "Of course not, Eli. It was a very polite transaction. I didn't even raise my voice. And I remembered to thank the tellers for their trouble. Why I even apologized for the inconvenience I caused them."

"Did you wear a mask?"

He waved his fine new handkerchief under my nose. "We are in no danger, Eli, I swear it. No one will come after us. I made a clean escape."

I laughed with relief and bounced on the bed. "That's enough money to get us to Tinville, Calvin! We won't have to do the orphan swindle after all. We can leave on the very next train."

I hugged myself with pleasure, thinking how much closer we were to Papa. Of course, it worried me some that Calvin had broken the law to help me on my way to Tinville, but I supposed he'd robbed banks before. Breaking the law was nothing new to the Gentleman Outlaw.

As for me, I figured I'd ease my conscience by making sure Calvin gave money to the poor and needy we were bound to meet along the way.

Sad to say, I soon discovered going to Tinville wasn't what the Gentleman Outlaw had in mind. Not yet. He said a hundred dollars was nothing compared to what he could get in the gambling halls and saloons of Alamosa.

"This is merely my stake," he said, "my entry into the game."

I tried to argue, but Calvin won me over with promises of diamond rings and gold stickpins, pearl-handled revolvers, fine horses, expensive hotels, the best dinners money could buy, champagne and oysters for breakfast. And candy. All the candy I could eat.

"Just imagine how proud your father will be when you step out of a first-class Pullman car," Calvin summed up, "dressed in fine clothes and carrying yourself like a perfect gentleman."

Though I couldn't tell Calvin just how much such a thing would truly astonish my father, I went along with his grand plans. Greedy as it sounds, I liked the idea of being rich for a change. Sleeping on soft mattresses, eating good food, wearing fine clothes. Why, it was like a fairy tale. My reward for all I'd suffered at Aunt Mabel and Uncle Homer's house.

14

THAT EVENING, CALVIN AND I TOOK SEATS ON the hotel's front porch. It was so blasted hot I thought I'd die. My suit was wool and as itchy as poison ivy. My shirt was buttoned up tight and starched so stiff it would have stopped a bullet. The collar just about rubbed my neck raw every time I turned my head. I might as well have had my chin in a vise. For the first time since I'd given up dresses and petticoats, I hated my clothes.

"Stop fidgeting," Calvin hissed in my ear, "and look sorrowful. Remember you're grieving for your dearly departed mama and papa."

Since I truly missed Mama every day of my life, it shouldn't have been hard to obey Calvin, but the heat and dust and flies were so tiresome I couldn't do anything but squint and scowl and squirm.

Finally I poked Calvin. "Can't I go up to the room and see what Caesar's doing? Sure as shooting he's bored stiff."

Instead of answering, Calvin squeezed my hand so hard I thought he'd cracked my bones. "See who's coming, Elijah? Look sad."

A gang of ruffians were riding toward the hotel, raising dust, scattering chickens and pigs, yelling and laughing and cursing. It was clear they could scarcely wait to throw their money away on whiskey, women, and cards.

"They appear to be mighty mean," I whispered.

Calvin sneered. "Ignorant, drunken scalawags. I wager there isn't an ounce of intelligence in all of them combined."

By now the miners were tramping up the steps, heading toward the saloon. They passed by without giving us a glance, but they left behind a smell a skunk would have been hard pressed to equal.

A few minutes later, Calvin unfolded his long, elegant body from his chair and pushed the saloon door open sort of slow and cautious like he wasn't used to entering such places.

For a few seconds, he hovered on the threshold with me beside him, peering into the smoky depths. It was a scene to make a preacher weep. Ladies dancing and singing bawdy songs, men snorting whiskey like it was water and cussing each other with every breath they took. On the wall behind the bar was a picture of a lady as naked as Eve in the garden and twice as big as life. Lord, I couldn't look at her or the dancing ladies without being ashamed of my sex.

When Calvin was sure we'd been noticed, he moved cautiously through the crowd.

"Please don't buy any whiskey, brother," I begged, remembering what he'd told me to say. And meaning it too. "You promised Mama when she lay dying that you'd be good."

"Don't mention that angel's name here," said Calvin, pretending to wipe tears with his handkerchief.

"She's looking down from heaven right now," I sobbed. "She sees you itching to spend our inheritance on the devil's drink."

By now we'd reached the bar. The miners stepped aside, making room for us. It was obvious we had their attention as well as the bartender's. Taking in the black mourning bands tied around our upper arms, he asked what we fancied.

"A sarsaparilla for my brother," Calvin said softly, "and a whiskey for me."

"No," I wept, warming to my part. "You promised not to touch it. You know what whiskey does to you, Calvin."

Nobody but a squint-eyed miner paid any attention to me. "What's the matter with you, boy?" he asked. "A man's got a right to his whiskey. Your brother don't need no trouble from you."

The man next to the miner laughed. Peering down at me, he said, "Now don't you pay no mind to Old Bill here. The poor cuss don't know what he's talking about or where he is most of the time."

But Old Bill wasn't listening to his friend. All his attention was focused on the silver coin Calvin had given to the bartender.

After Calvin put the change in his pocket, Old Bill turned back to me. "Your brother must be a rich man, boy. Why, I reckon he could buy us all a round or two."

I widened my eyes to look as innocent as possible. "Oh no, sir," I whispered. "That's our dear departed Mama's money. Calvin's not supposed to spend one blessed cent of it for whiskey, but today he's so over-whelmed with grief he won't listen to me."

Lowering my voice, I moved as close to Old Bill as my nose could bear. "Just between you and me," I whispered, "I'm afraid Calvin's about to fall back into his old ways. Before long he'll start gambling and lose everything."

Hearing me go on and on, Calvin glanced at me in some surprise. It was all I could do not to laugh. To tell you the truth, I was beginning to enjoy myself. I'd always had a hankering to act in a play, but this was even better because I got to make up my lines as I went along. Didn't have to memorize a thing.

Old Bill grinned at his companion. "Well, now, boy," he said, "it seems to me this here's a free country. There ain't no law against either gambling or drinking, so if that's what your brother wants to do, why, he should just go right ahead and do it. Yes, sir, that's just what he should do!"

While Old Bill was talking, Calvin drank his first glass of whiskey. Or at least he seemed to. If you watched real close, you'd have caught him dumping it in the spittoon. Luckily he did it so fast I was the only one who noticed.

When Calvin commenced to cough and choke, Old Bill slapped him on the back and urged him to have another glass. "Whiskey's the best thing for what ails you," he said. "Danged if it ain't!"

At first Calvin apologized to me for every glass, but after his third whiskey, he ignored my pleas. His voice slurred, he swayed and hung onto the bar like a man in fear of being washed overboard. He was mighty convincing.

Finally Old Bill suggested a game of poker. "Oh, brother, brother," I wept. "Think of poor Mama up there with the angels weeping over you."

Calvin's eyes filled with tears. "I'll play for Mama," he sobbed. "I'll win for my poor dead mother."

I kept right on protesting, but of course it didn't do a speck of good. In no time, Calvin was sitting at a table with a gang of miners. He lost hand after hand. The little pouch got flatter and flatter.

"Calvin," I cried, genuinely upset. "You promised you wouldn't lose it all!"

The miners scowled at me. One muttered something about pesky little varmints. Another mumbled children should be drowned at birth like kittens.

Finally Calvin turned to me. Giving me a quick

wink, he said, "Go back to our room, Elijah. With you gone, perhaps my luck will change."

"No!" I grabbed for the pouch, not sure I was still acting, but Calvin whisked it out of my reach.

"You heard what I said, Elijah," he hissed. "Leave at once!"

I backed away from the table, sure I'd seen the last of my train fare to Tinville.

One of the dancing girls put her arm around me. "Poor little fellow," she said. "To think your brother would gamble your inheritance away. When he came through the door, he looked a perfect gentleman, but to my sorrow, I've learned few folks are what they seem."

Giving me a friendly kiss on the cheek, she returned to the gambling table. I stood there awhile, watching Calvin lay down more of our precious coins. The dancing girl was right. He wasn't what he seemed. But neither was I. In fact, if someone had come up to me at that moment and asked me who I was, I don't think I could have said. I wasn't Eliza Yates any more, that's all I knew.

Upstairs I found Caesar sound asleep on my bed, snoring as loud as Uncle Homer. When I sat down beside him, he opened one eye and wagged his tail.

"You're the only one of us that's genuine," I told him, shaking the paw he offered. "You're just what you seem. A good old mutt—nothing more, nothing less. But who am I?"

Caesar licked my face and grinned. If he could have talked, he would probably have said, "You're you, just like I'm me." But instead of answering, he closed his eyes and went back to sleep, snoring louder than ever. Which proves it must be easier to be a dog than a person. No vexing questions. Just food and sleep.

I stayed awake for a long, long time, thinking these and other thoughts, expecting to be jolted out of bed by shouts, blasphemies, and gunfire from the saloon, but all I heard was the normal ruckus—no more profanity than usual, lots of hollering, most of it good-natured drunkenness, and every now and then a stray shot in the street.

Just about the time I was falling asleep in spite of myself, Calvin flung open the door, laughing like he was fit to be tied.

"Well, well, it seems you didn't get yourself killed after all," said I, not wanting him to know I gave a tinker's tulip for his worthless hide.

"There was never any chance of that, Eli," Calvin said. "By the time I turned the tables, those jackasses were too drunk to suspect I was cheating. Even if they had, no one would have believed them. Folks said I was blessed."

Overcome by a spell of hilarity, he laughed himself to tears. "One of the dancing girls actually claimed she saw the ghost of my poor dead mother," he snorted, tickled silly with himself. "She said

Mama was hovering over me, guiding the winning cards into my hand."

Calvin went on boasting and bragging till there was barely enough space for us both in the same room. His conceit was downright outrageous.

When he finally ran out of long, fancy words, I asked about that little pouch of silver dollars.

Calvin slapped his thigh and went off into another apoplectic fit of glee. Pulling the bulging pouch out of his pocket, he dumped its contents on the bureau, then emptied his pockets, adding gold coins as well as nuggets to his winnings. "One thousand, five hundred and twenty-six dollars, Eli. What do you think of me and my schemes now?"

"We're rich," I whispered. "We're rich!"

Calvin gave me a grin so wide his teeth shone in the dim light like a row of tombstones. "The more games I won, the more they wanted to play. The greedy rogues were convinced my luck would run out eventually. Why, it seems to me—"

Sick of his bragging, I cut into Calvin's words with an important question. "Now that we're rich, can we leave for Tinville?"

"Not right away," Calvin said, busying himself stacking and sorting coins. "We'll buy first-class tickets to Durango tomorrow morning. I hear the pickings are even better there."

My heart sank. "But Calvin, I thought you were in a big hurry to find Sheriff Yates. Why, he could leave Tinville any day. You'd never know where he went, never find him, never get your revenge."

Calvin ran a hand through his hair, smoothing it back from his face till he looked more like a boy my age than a grown man. "I have to be ready for Yates," he said. "I have to be prepared. Have to buy a gun, have to learn . . ." His words drifted into silence like little puffs of smoke.

"Maybe you ought to give me some of that money I helped you win," I said, quick to take advantage of his momentary speechlessness. "I could buy my ticket and go on to Tinville without you. Just me and Caesar."

Calvin looked at me in disbelief. "But Eli, I need you for the orphan swindle. We're partners. You can't desert me. Not when we're on our way to becoming millionaires."

I felt rotten about letting Calvin down, but I was mighty anxious to find Papa. "I hate to say it, Calvin, but I don't altogether trust you. I want my share of our winnings now—before you lose it."

"I don't entirely trust you either, my fine little friend," said Calvin, drawing himself up all huffy and proud. "I'll give you your share when we arrive in Tinville," he went on. "Till then, I keep everything except your candy money."

So saying, he dropped a few coins into my out-stretched palm. "Sixty cents. That will buy enough candy to rot every tooth in your lying little head."

I pocketed the money, knowing full well Calvin would steal it back if he needed it. Tomorrow I'd hide it in my fancy new shoes. They were a sight tighter than my old ones.

15

IN THE GRAY LIGHT OF DAWN, CALVIN AND I walked down to the depot and bought two tickets to Durango. While we waited for the train to come, we drank the worst coffee ever brewed. It was so strong Calvin said you could float a silver dollar on the surface. I tried it, and he laughed when the coin sank.

"I was speaking in hyperboles," he said in that highfalutin way of his.

"Maybe you should give over your criminal ways and become a schoolmaster," I said darkly. I still hadn't forgiven him for refusing to give me my share of his winnings, calling me a liar, and keeping me from getting to Tinville.

"Not me," Calvin said, not even noticing my glum mood. "Doc Holliday used to practice a little dentistry on the side, but he told Father he found it tedious compared to gunfighting and card-playing."

"Safer, though," I muttered. "I expect teachers and dentists are more likely to live to old age than gamblers and gunfighters."

Calvin sighed. "Which is better, Elijah? To have a short, exciting life and die in a burst of fame and glory or to have a long, uneventful life and die in bed, unknown and unremembered?"

I puzzled over the question. "Does it have to be one or the other?" I asked finally. "Can't there be something in between?"

"Not for me," Calvin said. "I want my name to live long after my body has turned to dust."

"What do you expect to be remembered for?" I asked. Though I didn't want to come right out and say it, all I'd seen Calvin do so far was cheat and lie and pick pockets—not very memorable activities, in my opinion.

Calvin leaned toward me. "After I shoot Sheriff Yates, my name will blaze across the firmament like a shooting star."

He made a sweeping gesture to demonstrate his flight of glory. Unfortunately his arm encountered a tray stacked with dirty dishes. As crockery crashed to the floor, the ill-natured waitress who'd been holding the tray slung it at Calvin, knocking him clean off his chair. He landed with an attention-getting thud among the broken cups and saucers and plates, soiling his fine new clothes.

Not satisfied with that, the waitress grabbed a

broom and chased poor Calvin out the door, whacking him with such ferocity I feared she'd break every bone in his handsome body.

Caesar and I ran after him, followed by loud laughter and shouts from our fellow diners. "They'll remember you here, Calvin," I said. "That's for certain. Why, they might even write a song about you— the outlaw swept up to heaven by a broom."

Giving me a fierce look, Calvin brushed bits of egg and toast off his trousers. When it came to laughing at himself, the Gentleman Outlaw lacked a sense of humor.

By the time the train came huffing and puffing into the depot, Calvin had regained his dignity. He seemed especially pleased that most of the folks who'd found his misfortune so amusing were riding in third class and we were riding in first.

"I don't hear them laughing now," he said as we boarded the Pullman car.

I must say first class was everything Calvin had promised it would be and more. My first glimpse of the carved woodwork and stained glass near took my breath away. The floor was carpeted, and the seats resembled sofas in softness and size. Sitting in such comfort made the train's rocking and jolting easier to bear. There was room to stretch your legs too.

Even the boys who came through selling food and drink and newspapers and such were soft-spoken and polite. They didn't holler in your face the way they did in third class, and their merchandise was definitely higher in quality—and in price.

The only disappointment was considerable. I'd been looking forward to eating fancy food in even fancier surroundings, but the train had no dining car. If we wanted lunch and dinner, we'd have to take our chances in the eating houses along the tracks. Since it was more than an eight-hour ride to Durango, we didn't have much choice. A body has to eat to keep strong.

→>•◄←

As soon as we got to Durango, we headed down Main Street, looking for the grandest hotel in town. It didn't take long to find the Strater. Built of red brick, it towered above us, brand-new and promising unimaginable luxury.

"Wait here with Caesar," Calvin said. "I'll go in and rent a room."

Awed by what I could see of the lobby, I watched Calvin stride into its depths as if he'd been born there. In a few minutes he was back with a room key.

"There's a side entrance," he said, leading me around the corner. "If we take Caesar in this way, they might not notice him."

We got Caesar up two flights of stairs and down a long red-carpeted hall without anyone spotting him. Calvin opened the door to room 211 and hustled the dog inside.

The moment the door closed behind us, I flung

· 121 ·

myself on the nearest bed. It was the softest I'd ever lain on. Like all the furniture, it was made of walnut, and its high headboard was carved with leaves and vines and scrolls. The bureaus had marble tops, and there was a pretty little sofa under the window, the sort most women would put in a parlor and forbid anyone to sit on.

Red velvet drapes kept out the afternoon sunlight. The floor was carpeted. The walls were covered with flocked paper in a fancy pattern. A pretty picture of the mountains hung over the washstand.

Calvin sat down on his bed and smiled at me. "Now aren't you glad we stopped in Durango?"

As much as I liked the Strater, I'd rather have gone on toward Tinville. But I didn't want to make Calvin mad or hurt his feelings by saying that, so I shrugged and told him the Strater was a mighty grand hotel. "Almost too grand," I added. "The very air smells costly."

I glanced at Caesar, who was scratching his fleas on the pretty little sofa. I swear he took to luxury quicker than I did.

→>•<←

That evening we had dinner in the hotel dining room, where I devoured a steak more than half my weight. Too full to budge, I gazed at the molding on the walls and ceiling, the potted palms, the waiters tiptoeing around with trays of food, and all the pretty ladies and handsome gentlemen dressed so nicely and eating so politely.

Turning to Calvin, I stretched out my hand and asked him to pinch me. "I can't believe I'm sitting here eating my dinner. I swear I must be dreaming the whole thing. Even the steak I just ate."

Calvin smiled. "I'm pleased to see you appreciate the finer things in life, Eli. Perhaps my efforts to civilize you have not been in vain. You may grow up to be a gentleman after all."

There wasn't much chance of that happening, but I kept my thoughts to myself.

Calvin drank the last of his coffee and got to his feet. "Come along, Eli. It's time to select a saloon and make our entrance."

Reluctantly I left the dining room, casting one last admiring look at the pretty plaster garlands adorning the walls and ceiling. Maybe Calvin was right, maybe Tinville could wait a little longer. Why, for all I knew, Papa was long gone from there. He could be anywhere by now, even California.

Caesar was sitting outside the hotel, tied to a hitching post where we'd left him. He seemed glad to see the big steak bone I'd saved for him, especially since I'd made sure there was plenty of meat on it.

I perched on a rail beside Calvin and watched Caesar crunch that bone to nothing. "We better take him with us tonight," I said. "If he barks in our room, there's no telling what might happen to him."

Calvin sighed. "I suppose you're right, Eli, but I wish he were better groomed and not quite so odoriferous."

Much as I hated to admit it, Calvin had a point. Poor old Caesar wasn't what most folks would call a handsome dog. Nor did he smell especially good. But he had a noble nature that shone in his eyes. And that's all that mattered.

The three of us ambled down the street, following the crowd to the Silver Queen Saloon, a likely place for miners to spend their hard-earned wealth.

At the door I went into my act and begged Calvin not to break his promise to Mama. He responded with a little speech about whiskey's effect on sorrow. Caesar got into the spirit of things by whimpering most pitifully.

We'd no sooner made our way to the bar than a golden-haired lady touched my arm. "What a pity to waste such a pretty face on a boy," she murmured, but it was Calvin's broad shoulders she was eyeing.

"Yes, ma'am," Calvin murmured. "Elijah here is the image of our dear, departed mother. Every time I see his face, I'm reminded of her." His eyes filled with tears and he turned his head to hide them.

As the lady began sympathizing with Calvin, I tugged at his sleeve. "Let's go back to the hotel," I begged.

The lady gave me a nasty look behind Calvin's back, reminding me for all the world of Millicent.

"A shot of whiskey is what your brother needs," she said sweetly. "You'll see him smiling soon, just you wait."

The bartender was quick to provide a glass and a bottle. Calvin went through the motions of drinking, but, like the night before, he dumped the whiskey so fast no one saw but me. Soon he was sitting at a card table, as bleary-eyed and slur-tongued as any fool.

The lady perched herself on Calvin's knee, whispering in his ear and kissing him in the mushiest way, but every now and then, I caught her winking at the big-time gambler dealing the cards. Like the mysterious stranger we'd met in Pueblo, he wore a fancy diamond stickpin in his ruffled shirt and his fingers sparkled with rings. From the hard way he glanced at Calvin and me, I knew *he'd* never help a poor boy.

My fear of the dealer must have shown in my voice for Calvin looked right vexed at the way I was begging him to quit before he lost everything. I guess he knew I wasn't playacting.

The lady frowned. She'd lost patience with me a long time ago. "Maybe you should send your little brother home to bed," she suggested. "It appears to me he's up past his bedtime."

Calvin looked at me thoughtfully. "I believe you may be right," he told the lady.

Putting all the iron I could muster into my voice, I said, "I'm not leaving unless you come with me."

Calvin pulled me close and whispered, "Do as I

say, Elijah. I understand this situation better than you do."

"You and your airs," I muttered. "Sometimes I think Miss Nellie was right about you, Calvin Featherbone. You don't have the sense you were born with."

Fed up with watching him make a fool of himself, I stalked out of the saloon with Caesar at my heels. Behind me, the lady laughed and some of the ruffians at the card table joined in, but I paid them no heed. Let Calvin do what he pleased. I wanted no more of him.

Halfway back to the Strater, I saw something that changed my mind fast. A man lurched out of a saloon just ahead, followed by two others. Flattening myself against the side of a building, I watched Roscoe, Baldy, and Shovel Face stagger past. The three of them were heading in the direction of the Silver Queen.

There was nothing to do but cut down an alley and hope I got there first. No matter how vexed I was, I didn't want anything bad to happen to Calvin.

ONE THING YOU SHOULD NEVER DO IS TAKE a shortcut in a strange town. The alley I ran down had a fence across the end. Even if I could have climbed over it, Caesar couldn't have followed me. We turned and ran back to the street, but we'd lost precious time. Before we even got in sight of the Silver Queen, we heard gunshots.

Inside the saloon, chairs and bottles were flying through the air, accompanied by fisticuffs and blasphemy vile enough to curdle milk. The smoke was so thick I couldn't see Calvin anywhere, but that didn't stop Caesar and me from going in to rescue him. Like Calvin, I don't have the sense I was born with. It must have leaked out my ears when I was no more than a baby.

From somewhere in the fire and brimstone, I heard a voice holler, "Come out and face me like a man, you lily-livered, no good, worthless son of . . ."

I won't tell you what else he said, but when the smoke cleared I saw Roscoe standing in the middle of the room, a gun in his hand. Backing him up were Shovel Face and Baldy.

"You won't cheat me again, Featherbone," Roscoe bellowed, waving his gun. "Nor nobody else neither."

Calvin was standing by the card table, his chair on the floor behind him, his face as white as his shirt front. The dealer was on his feet, gun drawn and smoking. I reckon he'd already taken a shot at Roscoe. As for the pretty lady, all I saw of her was a bit of frilly red lace sticking out from behind an overturned table. I guess she wasn't crazy enough about Calvin to risk getting killed.

While I stood there taking in the scene, Caesar let out a fierce snarl and hurled himself at Roscoe. Before the scoundrel knew what was happening, Caesar was standing over him, slavering like a wolf ready to rip his throat out.

Sizing up the situation, I ran to Calvin's side and pointed at Roscoe, who was rolling around on the floor with Caesar as if they were wrestling. "Don't believe a word that lying scalawag says," I sobbed. "Mr. Suggs tried to bamboozle us out of our inheritance back in Kansas. Why, he stole our mama's farm and broke her heart. He might as well have shot her dead like he's aiming to do to Calvin now."

My tears swayed the crowd to Calvin's side. Every man and woman turned on Roscoe and his boys with shouts and curses and cries of "Shame!" In a trice, that gang of no-goods were scampering toward the door.

Shaking off my dog, Roscoe paused just long enough to yell, "I won't forget this, Featherbone! Sooner or later, I'll get you and that little varmint alone somewheres and then we'll see, oh yes, we will!"

With that, the doors swung shut and Roscoe was gone. Satisfied, Caesar trotted back to me, panting a little, and dropped the seat of Roscoe's trousers at my feet. Folks laughed and cheered. The piano player suggested hanging the rag over the bar as a souvenir of the night's merriment, and the bartender obliged.

In a few minutes things were back to normal. I guess the customers were used to brawls and destruction.

But I wasn't. And neither was Caesar. We found us a nice quiet corner out of everybody's way and waited for Calvin to finish playing. The pretty lady hung over him, trying to peek at his cards, but he kept them close to his chest. Every now and then she flashed a smile at me as if to apologize for the harsh words she'd spoken earlier, but I was too weary to return the courtesy.

I watched Calvin lose hand after hand till it seemed I'd saved his life only to see him gamble away our fortune. Just as I was about to fling myself at him and beg him to quit, he started winning. If he was cheating, I couldn't tell, nor could anybody else. Except for the dealer, the folks gathered around the table seemed happy to see Calvin's luck change. Especially the pretty lady, who hopped all over him like a flea, kissing him and stroking his hair and whispering in his ear.

When the last man quit, Calvin raked in his winnings and turned to me, his face flushed and his eyes fever-bright. "Are you happy, little brother?"

I got to my feet, too tired to do anything but nod. "Can we go back to the hotel now?"

"The night is still young, my handsome darling," said the pretty lady, caressing Calvin's face as if she were blind and couldn't see what he looked like without touching him.

"Alas," Calvin murmured, "I promised dear Mama to take good care of my little brother. I fear I've neglected my duty and kept him up long past his bedtime. Good night to you all."

Tipping his hat, the Gentleman Outlaw took my hand as if I were a helpless child and moved toward the door, with Caesar trotting along beside us.

The pretty lady came along with us, clinging to Calvin's arm and promising him all sorts of things. Behind her, the dealer watched, one hand resting lightly on his revolver and the other smoothing his mustache, looking for all the world like a villain right out of a Western story.

When Calvin continued to decline as courteously as a knight from olden days, the pretty lady finally lost her temper and called my companion a stupid boy, a fool, and other things too nasty to repeat.

"I know you was cheating," she screeched. "Next time I'll catch you at it. Then Jack McGraw will shoot you dead! He don't like cheats at his table!"

So saying, she took off down the dark street, pausing every now and then to shout a few more unladylike things at us. I swear I was tempted to sic Caesar on her. He'd have gladly ripped her frills to shreds.

"Step lively, Eli," Calvin hissed, yanking me along by one arm. "It appears we've made yet another enemy."

Calvin, Caesar, and I ran to the hotel, slipped in the side entrance, and raced up the steps to our room. After we shut and locked the door, Calvin went to the window and peered down into the street.

"Is McGraw coming?" I whispered, too afraid to go see for myself.

Calvin shook his head and pulled the drapes shut. Lighting the lamp, he busied himself counting his winnings. It looked like a goodly amount.

"Now we have two evil men to worry about," I said. "Roscoe Suggs and Jack McGraw. It seems to me we'd better move on to Tinville while we're still alive."

Calvin stretched out on his bed and stared at the ceiling. "The Silver Queen isn't the only saloon in Durango," he said.

"Jack McGraw was watching you real close," I said. "Like that lady, I wager he knew you were cheating. He's bound to tell others."

Calvin surprised me by agreeing. "Perhaps you're right," he said. "From what I hear, Silverton has a goodly number of saloons and gambling halls."

"Why can't we go straight on to Tinville?"

"Oh, Lord," Calvin sighed. "I wish I'd never heard the name of that town. You've worn it out saying it so often."

"But—"

"No 'buts,' Eli." Turning his back, Calvin blew out the lamp and prepared for bed.

Without saying another word, I undressed too and slid under my soft blanket. I was too worn down to argue. Wouldn't do any good anyway. It was clear Calvin had made up his mind. The most I could hope for was to be run out of Silverton as fast as we'd been run out of Durango.

17

T HE NEXT MORNING WE ATE A GOOD BREAK-
fast at the Strater, paid our bill, and headed
down Main Street to the depot. Everything looked
clean and shiny in the sunlight, including the train
itself. Pure white steam billowed from its smoke-
stack, rising up like a cloud against the blue sky.
Steam hissed out from under the locomotive too. It
was huffing and puffing, just raring to go.

The dark green cars were already filling with passengers. Families and fancy ladies, a man of the
cloth, several gamblers, assorted miners. It seemed
like half of Durango was heading north to Silverton.
Those that were staying crowded the platform, waving and shouting to the ones who were going.

"First class again," Calvin said, guiding me to a
Pullman car. "It's a three-hour journey, so we might
as well avoid the hoi polloi and travel in luxury. We
can afford it."

With Caesar lying quietly at our feet, Calvin and I sat back in our plush seats and watched Durango slip away into the past, already no more than a vivid dream.

The tracks ran along beside the Animas River, short for *el Rio de las Animas Perdidas,* according to Calvin. The name rolled off his tongue like poetry, but when he told me its meaning, I shivered. *The river of lost souls*—that's what those pretty Spanish words signified. I wondered how it got such a grim name. And hoped it didn't bode ill for us.

After a while, the train began climbing, twisting and turning, following the very edge of a steep cliff. The river dropped farther and farther below us. Soon I had to lean out the window to see the water churning over boulders at the bottom of a chasm. Lost souls . . . the name made more sense when I looked down at the river from this height.

Beyond the Animas, the mountains rose up, high and stern and pointed, bearded with pines. Big white clouds hung motionless above the peaks. The sky was the bluest I'd ever seen. Except for the everlasting cinders and smoke from the locomotive, the air was fresh and pure. It was a fine ride, made even better by a plush dining car and a delicious meal of pheasant, elk, and buffalo.

In Silverton, we took a room at the Grand Hotel, on Greene Street, an establishment nearly as fine as the Strater. The food in the dining room was good and plentiful, and I soon got into the habit of eating steak tender enough to cut with my fork. Even developed a taste for oysters, which Calvin said would put hair on my chest—highly unlikely, I thought.

As Calvin had predicted, saloons and gambling halls were plentiful in Silverton. The first thing we did when we entered one was take note of the dealer. If he seemed the equal of Jack McGraw, we tried another place. No sense taking chances when you don't need to.

To insure our good luck, Calvin devised new methods of cheating. Besides his quick fingers and polite ways, he kept an ace up his sleeve and marked his cards. He also bought himself a pretty glass ring that looked like a diamond but was even better because he could turn it to reflect other players' cards. Of course, he wasn't above using me to send him silent signals. Not too many men paid heed to a pitiful orphan hanging around the table. Night after night, our winnings grew.

→>-◄←

One evening while we were enjoying dinner in the hotel dining room, Calvin surprised me by bringing up the subject of his father. He hadn't said much about Mr. Featherbone, Senior, since I'd questioned his honesty in card-playing way back in Pueblo.

"I imagine Father spent a lot of time in this town," he said, looking around as if he expected to see old Featherbone's ghost lingering in a corner. "What I wouldn't give to have known him better, to have traveled with him, to have been his partner."

Calvin's fists tightened and a little muscle in his cheek twitched. "Thanks to Sheriff Yates, I have been denied that opportunity."

I leaned across the table and asked a question I'd been puzzling over for a long time. "How do you know Sheriff Yates killed your father, Calvin? Who told you?"

Reaching into the inside pocket of his coat, Calvin pulled out a tattered envelope. Opening it carefully, he removed a letter which had been unfolded and refolded so many times it was torn along the creases. "Read this, Eli."

I spread the fragile paper on the table. "*My dere Miz Fetherbone*," I read,

> *With grate sorroe I take pen in hand to tell you of yore husbands crool and untimly deth. On February 10th 1887 he was shot in the back in cold blud by the sherif of Tinville on account of him calling the sherif a cheet wich is the truth. Alfred Yates is the sherif's name. He took all the munny yore pore unforchinat husband had. This is all I have to say, x-cept the sherif is a wicked man that shood be kilt for his trechery.*
>
> *Yore husbands frend*

Before I raised my eyes, I took a deep breath. Until now, I hadn't known Sheriff Yates's Christian name was Alfred. By a strange coincidence, my father's Christian name was also Alfred. Much as I feared to admit it, it was beginning to look like Calvin and I were searching for the same man after all.

When I could trust myself to speak, I asked Calvin who sent the letter. "There's no signature."

"What does it matter who sent it? The truth is my father is dead and I, his only living kin, swore a vow on my mother's grave to avenge his murder."

Calvin's face was pale, and his voice shook. For the first time I felt I was seeing his true self, a boy not much older than me who had made a solemn promise. One he could not break, even if he wanted to, without dishonoring himself.

"You're scared, aren't you?" I whispered, just blurting the words out without thinking. "That's why you're hanging round here instead of going on to Tinville."

Calvin snatched the letter back and refolded it carefully, scowling at me all the while. "Of course I'm not scared," he said fiercely. "I know how to handle a gun."

"You don't even have a gun," I said. "Why, I bet you never shot one in your whole entire life."

Calvin got up so quick his chair fell over. The noise won us the attention of everyone in the dining room, including a waiter who almost dropped a tray full of steaming dinners.

"If you were a man instead of a puny little Nancy-boy," Calvin snarled, "I'd beat you senseless for insulting me."

Ignoring the stares and whispers, Calvin whirled around and headed for the exit.

I sat at the table for a moment, knowing I'd pushed Calvin too far this time. I was usually better at guessing his moods and accommodating myself to them.

"Shall I put the dinner on your hotel bill, son?" the waiter asked, hovering over me.

"Yes," I said, getting to my feet. "Room 112."

Without looking at anyone, I slunk out of the dining room and went in search of Calvin.

I caught up with him and Caesar a block or two down the street. "I'm sorry, Calvin," I hollered at his back. "I didn't mean to insult you, I just said what I was thinking."

But Calvin wouldn't look at me. Nor would he speak. He went on walking, faster and faster, his coattails flying out with every step.

"Where are you going?" I shouted.

Without answering, Calvin crossed the road, strode into a gun store, and marched up to the counter. "I want the best pistol you have, and hang the cost," he said to the startled clerk, who'd been dozing over a Deadwood Dick story.

The clerk spit a stream of tobacco juice onto the floor, totally missing the spittoon, and leaned over the gun case. "That would be this here Colt forty-five," he said. "The Peacemaker, they call it."

"May I see it?"

When the clerk opened the case, I sidled up to Calvin and stood beside him so I could see the guns too. They reminded me of snakes—beautiful but deadly.

The clerk handed Calvin the Colt as if it were a sacred object. "Pure ivory handles," he murmured, "and a special embossed holster made from the finest leather."

Calvin weighed the pistol, sighted, squeezed the trigger, spun the chamber. Either I was wrong about him never having had a gun, or he knew how to look good with one in his hand.

"I can let her go for a hundred dollars," said the clerk.

Calvin frowned. "I told you I don't care about the price. If this is the best you have, then it's the one I want."

Without hesitating, Calvin pulled out his money pouch and laid ten gold eagles on the counter.

"I'll have to charge another two or three dollars for ammunition," the clerk apologized.

Calvin buckled the holster and handed the clerk four silver dollars. In exchange, he received enough bullets to shoot every soul in Silverton at least once.

Outside the store, the street lay in shadow but the upper stories of buildings caught the sunlight. Windowpanes reflected the red sky as if the whole town were burning. Horses stood at hitching rails, flipping their tails and exchanging whinnies. From Blair Street came the sounds of piano music, laughter, shouts, and a gunshot or two. The saloons were filling. It was time to pick one for our act.

"How do I look, Eli?" Calvin asked coldly. "Am I professional enough for you now?"

He looked like a boy playing a part in a play, I thought, but there wasn't any sense getting him riled up with the truth again.

"I just hope you know how to use that gun," I said. "Now that you're armed, you're a fair target for anybody who cares to shoot you."

Without speaking, Calvin smoothed his curls and swung off toward Blair Street. I trotted along beside him, and Caesar followed close behind. Another long night of gambling lay ahead. Drunken louts bumping me, perfumed ladies hanging on Calvin, loud music, cigar smoke, a sarsaparilla or two.

I wondered what Mama would say if she looked down from heaven and saw me, her only child and daughter, wearing boys' clothes and knowing more about the inside of a saloon than a church or a schoolhouse. She wouldn't be pleased, that was for certain.

As for myself, I wasn't too pleased either. Once

I'd enjoyed accompanying Calvin in his playacting, but now I was just plain weary of it. All I wanted to do was get to Tinville and keep Calvin from killing Papa. Or Papa from killing him.

18

AS THINGS TURNED OUT, I WASN'T DESTINED to play my part in the orphan act much longer. A couple of nights later, Caesar and I were sitting on the sidewalk outside the Olympic Saloon. Calvin was inside playing the fool at the faro table. All those unwashed clothes and bodies had given me a headache. I was glad to have a few moments to be still and admire the stars shining high in the night sky, untouched by the ugliness down below them.

Just as I was waxing poetical, a ruckus erupted behind me. Calvin came running out the saloon door, followed by a stream of curses and gunfire. I knew better than to waste time asking questions. Caesar and I did what we'd learned. We raced after Calvin, ducking down alleys, hiding in shadows, doing our best to lose the angry crowd chasing us. Bullets whizzed past my head, buzzing like angry hornets, but thank the Lord nobody was sober enough to shoot straight.

When we decided it was safe to stop running, we hunkered down behind a fence and practiced breathing normally.

"How come you didn't shoot back?" I asked Calvin, as soon as I had enough wind to speak. "You haven't even drawn your pistol."

He glanced at his holster as if he'd forgotten it was there. "I told you I avoid gunplay," he said kind of stiffly.

I had a good idea Calvin wasn't telling the truth about his reasons for not shooting, but I didn't want to set him off again, not when he was feeling so touchy. "What happened in the saloon?" I asked. "Did someone catch on to your tricks?"

Calvin sighed. "A miner I cheated a few days ago turned up in the crowd. Unfortunately I didn't notice him watching me, and I grew careless with my glass ring."

"Does this mean we're leaving Silverton?"

"I'm afraid so," Calvin said. "We'll depart on the first stage in the morning." He sighed again, louder and harder than before. "I fear we won't be traveling first class for some time, Eli. I had to choose between my winnings and my life. I chose the latter and left the gold on the table."

He reached into his pocket and held out his hand. Five silver dollars and a few coins gleamed in the moonlight.

"That's it?" I stared at the paltry sum in disbelief. "That's all we've got?"

"I told you it was either take the money and die or leave it and live."

"In other words, you decided you weren't quite ready to blaze that path across the firmament."

Calvin ignored my sarcasm and began walking toward the stage depot, taking care to keep in the shadows. Caesar and I followed him, but I swear if I'd had a grain of sense, I would have demanded my share of those coins and taken a later stage. Just Caesar and me. No more Gentleman Outlaw and his cheating ways.

But as I've already told you, I'm totally lacking in sense. Besides I could no more have left Calvin than I could have left Caesar. They both needed me. The only difference was Caesar knew it and Calvin didn't.

As we passed the Grand Hotel, I stopped and grabbed Calvin's sleeve. "Where are you going? We have to pay our bill and get our belongings."

Calvin gave me a look so long he might have been measuring me for something. A coffin maybe. "Eli, we don't have enough money to pay the bill," he said. "As for our belongings, what do we have but the clothes on our backs?"

When we got to the depot, we huddled on a bench in the shadows at the back until it was time to board the stagecoach. Calvin bought our tickets and hustled me inside. I expected someone to complain about Caesar, but the three miners sharing one seat were already half-asleep. The lady sitting beside Calvin was too busy chatting to a handsome gambler to notice my dog. The gambler paid no heed to anything but the lady. So it seemed Caesar was safe. At least for now.

Before we departed, at least six more miners climbed up on top of the coach. They clung to the sides like shipwrecked sailors, passing the time in the usual fashion—singing, laughing, hollering, and cursing.

The miners inside the coach were soon snoring away, filling the air with unpleasant odors. Making a face, the lady pressed a hanky to her nose and went on talking to the gambler. Calvin and Caesar fell asleep. Ignoring the whole bunch, I stuck my head out the window and watched Silverton shrink to nothing behind us.

As soon as we left the flat ground outside town, the excitement began. The Red Mountain toll road was built on the edge of a sheer cliff. What's more, it was narrow and full of twists and turns. The mountains were so high I couldn't tell how far up we were. Which was probably a good thing.

To make matters even worse, the driver acted as if the hounds of hell were chasing us. Cracking the whip and cursing the horses, he swerved around curves, bouncing and swaying. At any moment, I expected the coach to careen off the road and plunge down the mountainside, carrying us all to certain death.

By the time we got to Bear Creek Falls, our first stop, I was so weak-kneed I fell out of the coach and landed on my face, a mishap the miners found uncommonly funny. Calvin helped me up and Caesar licked my face, but I'd ripped a hole in the knee of my good pants and hurt my pride as well.

The only thing in that godforsaken place was a hotel. Since the wind was blowing fierce, we followed the other passengers inside. While the miners treated each other to whiskey and beer, Calvin bought strong black coffee and a roll for each of us. I shared my roll with Caesar, who was glad to get a bite.

When the driver had changed horses, he summoned us back to the coach and we were off again. Even though it was just the end of August, it commenced to snow. The air filled with whirling flakes as big as goose feathers, but it was downhill all the way to Ouray and nothing slowed the driver. How those miners stayed on top of the coach, I can't guess. Inside we were all flung about, jolted this way and that till there wasn't an unbruised place on my body.

In Ouray, we discovered we'd missed the daily train to Tinville. It was late afternoon and the snow had turned to cold rain, blowing so hard it stung my face and cut right through my suit jacket. It seemed our luck had definitely taken a bad turn.

I looked at Calvin. "What are we going to eat?" I asked. "Where are we going to sleep?"

Leading me into a dingy restaurant where roaches outnumbered paying customers, Calvin began searching his pockets, a process which yielded a few cents. "What did you do with all that candy money I gave you?" he asked.

For the first time I regretted spending every cent I'd had on long, chewy strings of licorice, fist-sized sour balls, and peppermint drops so sweet they made my jaws ache in memory. "What do you think I did with it?" I muttered.

Calvin sighed and looked at the coins on the table. It was enough for two plates of beans and a few chunks of stale bread.

I choked down a mouthful of beans and flattened a roach with my fist at the same time—a good trick, I thought, but Calvin didn't even notice.

At my feet, Caesar thumped the floor with his tail, raising dust and fleas, and I slipped him the rest of my beans. If I ate another one, I'd explode.

"Maybe you should see that man about a dog," I said, remembering the mysterious bag of silver Calvin had produced back in Alamosa.

"I'm afraid he has no more dogs for me," Calvin said.

"How about if I play my harmonica in the saloon across the street? If I get enough money, we could start up a game of three-card monte. Why, before you know it, we'll be rich again."

Calvin just sat there contemplating the roach

crawling across his empty plate. I'd never seen him so dejected.

"What if you sold that pistol?" I asked.

His hand went to the Colt's handle. "No," he said. "I think the time has come to use it."

"You mean rob a bank?" I drew in my breath and held it, too scared to let it go. Once I'd have been excited at the prospect of becoming a true outlaw, but by now I'd lost faith in Calvin. It seemed to me if he held up a bank we'd surely be caught. Shot maybe. Sent to jail. Hanged.

Calvin didn't answer. Just got to his feet and walked slowly toward the door. He had the look of a man going to his death.

I ran after him and grabbed his sleeve. "Listen here," I said, "I don't think bank robbery is a good idea, Calvin. Let's try begging first. Just look at that saloon. Why, it's bound to be full of miners who'd take pity on a poor orphan boy."

Calvin shrugged me off and stepped outside. It was dark now and raining hard. "I told you I was an outlaw," he said. "Don't you think I know how to rob a bank?"

"No," I said. "I don't think you know the least thing about such matters. Cheating and playing tricks is all you're good at. And talking like you swallowed a dictionary." I was thinking of Miss Nellie when I spoke, remembering the things she'd said and wishing I'd paid more heed to her words. It was clear now she'd known Mr. Calvin T. Featherbone a sight better than I had.

We stood there in the freezing rain glowering at each other. Caesar looked from me to Calvin and back again, wagging his tail in a puzzled way. Just up the street was the Beaumont Hotel, the equal of the Strater back in Durango. I suppose the poor dog was wondering why we weren't heading there. Like me, he'd grown accustomed to luxury beyond his lot in life.

Suddenly Calvin's face lit up. "Look, Eli," he said, pointing at the hitching rail in front of the Last Chance Saloon. "Do you see what I see?"

I stared at the three horses, trying to figure out what Calvin was getting at.

"They belong to Roscoe and his boys," Calvin said.

"Are you sure?"

"Of course I'm sure." Sounding more like himself, Calvin told me to follow him.

"Calvin," I whimpered, "you aren't fixing to steal them, are you? Horse theft's a hanging offense."

"Those rogues stole *my* horse," Calvin muttered, untying the best of the bunch, a swaybacked roan with a mean look in its eye. "He was a pure Arabian, worth three or four times as much as these three nags put together. The ruffians must have sold him!"

In no time at all, Calvin was on the roan's back, I

was on the Appaloosa, and we were leading the third, a cantankerous gray. With Caesar running beside us, we left Ouray in a cold rain and rode into the hills, heading for Tinville at last.

19

WHEN WE'D PUT WHAT WE HOPED WAS A safe distance between us and Ouray, Calvin and I found a little cave to hole up in. We hobbled the horses and carried Roscoe's and his friends' bedrolls inside. Calvin scraped together enough dry brush to start a fire. Except for the smell of Roscoe's blankets, the cave was right cozy.

It seemed neither Calvin nor I had a thing to say to the other. Our clothes were soaked through to our skins. We were cold, hungry, bone tired, and stiff from sitting in the saddle for hours. Without even looking at each other, we rolled up in the blankets and endeavored to fall asleep as soon as possible. If this was the outlaw life I'd once dreamed of leading, I wanted no more of it.

Sometime around dawn, I woke up. Calvin was still sleeping. He looked a sight worse for wear, and I suppose I did too. The rain had shrunk our nice wool jackets and trousers. Their black dye had run onto our white shirts, turning them a limp, streaky gray. It would have taken a day's ironing to press the wrinkles out. On top of everything else, Calvin's face was stubbled with whiskers, one thing at least I'd never have to worry about.

Calvin must have sensed I was watching him, because he stirred and opened his eyes. The fire had burned to ashes, and the air was damp and cold. It was still raining. I could hear water dripping and gurgling outside. I had a feeling it wouldn't stop till the world was drowned and us with it.

"Well, Eli," Calvin said, "we seem to be back where we started. Sleeping on the cold, hard ground. And this time, not a dollar between us. As usual, I've made a miserable mess of things."

I nodded glumly. It made no sense to argue. For once, Calvin Thaddeus Featherbone, Junior, was telling the truth.

Since he seemed to be in the mood for honest answers, I leaned toward him, daring him to look me in the eye and lie. "Tell me something, Calvin. Are you known as the Gentleman Outlaw to anyone but yourself?"

Calvin poked the fire till he coaxed a little flame to spring up, then shook his head slowly. "Those miserable horses and a cheap pocket watch are the only items I've ever stolen," he whispered, keeping his head down as if he were ashamed to admit he'd never committed a crime. "My entire knowledge of outlawing comes from Western novels and Father's letters."

He raised his head then and gave me a fierce look. "I am, however, a gentleman through and through. I've never lied about *that*."

"But what about that hundred dollars you got in Alamosa?" I asked. "If you didn't steal it, where on earth did it come from?"

Calvin added some tinder to the fire and sighed. "I wired my grandfather for money. Although he complied, he told me not to expect any more financial assistance. If I planned to waste my life as my father did, he said, I'd have to do it without his support."

Raising his head, he gazed at me with eyes as sorrowful as Caesar's. "Before you wash your hands of me," he said, "I swear I intend to earn my sobriquet in Tinville. After I kill Sheriff Yates, people will truly speak of me as the Gentleman Outlaw."

"Oh, Calvin," I said, "please don't go shooting at that sheriff. Remember what Miss Pearl told you way back in Kansas?"

"When she accused me of being nothing but a greenhorn boy?" Calvin's face darkened with anger. "I'm not likely to forget an insult of that magnitude."

"But, Calvin, it's true, you just said so yourself." I grabbed his shoulders and peered into his eyes.

"You don't know anything about shooting and killing. You'll end up with a bullet through your heart."

Calvin pulled away from me and scrambled to his feet. Using the advantage of his height, he glowered down at me. "I promised Mother," he said. "I swore on her grave. Do you expect me to break a vow like that?"

"Is shooting Sheriff Yates going to bring your father back to life?"

"You know nothing about the southern code of honor," Calvin said, his voice going icy cold with contempt.

"I know more than you do about the foolishness of such vows," I said. "It's you who'll die in the dust like a dog, not the sheriff. That won't do anybody a speck of good, except the undertaker and the coffin maker. They'll make a tidy profit from your death."

Calvin smoothed his coat but it had shrunk to a point where nothing could help its appearance. "Just wait and see. Right is on my side, Eli, and right makes might."

I spit into the fire and made it sizzle. "If you're so hell-bent on dying, go right ahead. See if I cry at your funeral!" I almost screamed the words.

Without looking at Calvin again, I rolled up my blankets, grabbed my saddle, and staggered out of the cave, hoping to hide the tears running down my face. It wasn't just my father I was crying for. It was Calvin too. I didn't want to see either of them get killed.

Calvin followed me and slung his saddle on the roan. "When we reach Tinville," he said, with a haughty little sniff, "we'll see whose funeral it will be."

Off we rode into the endless rain, with poor old Caesar trailing along behind, bellies empty and too mad to talk to each other.

→>•◄←

Just before sunset, we reined in at the edge of a cliff. The rain had finally stopped, but the sky was still dark and clouds hid the mountaintops. Down below was a good-sized town. From where we sat, we saw a train pulling out of a depot, smoke as black as night pluming out behind it.

"That must be Ridgway," Calvin said, speaking for the first time. "If we only had money, we could ride the train from there to Tinville."

"We could sell the horses," I said, "and the gun too."

Calvin gave me a sharp look as if he suspected I was trying to trick him. "You know I can't part with the Colt," he said crossly.

Without saying more, we made our way down a steep trail and entered Ridgway, yet another muddy town full of stray dogs and saloons. After a short search, we found a run-down livery on a back street where nobody seemed to care about the legalities of horse selling as long as we were willing to accept a low price.

The money was enough for two third-class tickets to Tinville, as well as a big plate of beans apiece at the depot restaurant. I fought the flies for every morsel and then gave Caesar the plate to lick. He cleaned it up so well I doubt anyone bothered to wash it.

After that, there was nothing to do but sit on an old baggage cart and wait for the next train to Tinville.

I glanced at Calvin perched beside me, fingering that murderous Colt, his face pale and scared. I wanted to be as honest with him as he'd been with me, but the words stuck in my throat.

I ended up keeping my secrets, hoping things would work themselves out in some unforeseen way with nobody getting hurt.

20

ALVIN AND I FOUND A SEAT IN A CAR crowded with folks from every nation on earth and made ourselves as comfortable as possible. Caesar lay down at my feet and sighed a weary sigh. Following the horses for so many miles had plumb worn him out, and he was glad for a rest.

Our luck took another turn for the worse somewhere between Buena Vista and Tinville. We'd been on the train for hours, rocking to and fro, too hungry to talk. Calvin fell asleep first, and I soon dozed off myself. It was Caesar's growl that woke me up.

I opened one eye, aiming to quiet Caesar with a nudge from my shoe, and who did I see coming down the aisle but Roscoe, Baldy, and Shovel Face. Swaying with the train, they were bumping and jostling folks and sometimes falling into ladies' laps, deliberately I was sure. They hadn't seen us yet, but unless one of their outraged victims shot them first, they soon would.

I dug my elbow into Calvin's side. He woke, swearing like a gentleman, which is to say his profanities didn't violate the rules of grammar.

"Hush up and look what's coming our way," I hissed.

Calvin and Roscoe saw each other at the same time. "There he is!" Roscoe hollered, pointing straight at Calvin. "Not only is that rogue a cheating tinhorn gambler, but he's a horse thief as well. I got the poster right here to prove it!"

Roscoe paused to pry a wadded piece of paper out of his pocket, no easy task when your pants fit as tight as his. Fearing the mood of the passengers might turn against us, Calvin and I took advantage of the situation. Without a word we ran down the aisle, dragging Caesar after us, and rushed into the next car, heading as fast as we could for the rear of the train.

Without meaning to, we bumped and banged folks right and left. A chorus of curses smoked the air around us, but we kept going, apologizing as we went.

On the back platform, Calvin started clambering up a ladder to the roof. I was about to follow when I remembered Caesar. I couldn't very well go off and leave him, not when he'd been so brave and loyal and true.

"Calvin," I yelled, to be heard over the noise of the train. "What about Caesar?"

The Gentleman Outlaw peered over the edge of the roof, white-faced and hanging on with all his strength. "Boost him up," he hollered. "I'll grab his paws and pull him the rest of the way."

I grabbed the dog and tried to hoist him up the ladder toward Calvin's outstretched hands, but at that moment the door flew open. Out came Roscoe, belly first, a pistol in his hand. I closed my eyes, sure he meant to shoot all three of us, but he shoved me aside and climbed up the ladder after Calvin.

"Featherbone!" he bellowed. "Stop or I'll shoot you dead! There's reward money on your miserable head, and I aim to collect it!"

I heard Calvin yell, "No obese ignoramus is going to hand me over to the authorities!"

Then there was shooting and more yelling and cursing. Next thing I knew, Roscoe was wrestling Calvin down the ladder. The Gentleman Outlaw was still swearing and struggling, but he wasn't bleeding. It appeared Roscoe had missed him altogether.

When Roscoe was almost down, he made the mistake of sticking his big old rear end right in Caesar's face. It's no wonder my dog sank his teeth into it. From the way he hung on, it seemed Caesar wanted a piece of Roscoe's trousers to replace the one he'd left behind in Durango.

Roscoe let out a bellow of pure rage, and Shovel Face aimed his gun at Caesar. He would have killed my dog right then and there, but I threw myself in front of Caesar and begged Shovel Face not to shoot.

Baldy sniggered and said, "Go ahead, pard', plug 'em both. They ain't nothing but no-count little old varmints anyways. The world would be well shut of the pair of 'em."

Shovel Face squinted down the barrel of his gun as if he was trying to decide which of us to aim at first. Before he made up his mind, the train conductor stepped out on the platform. He had a couple of hard-looking men with him, Pinkerton thugs, I guessed, hired to protect the railroad against the likes of Calvin and me.

"What's going on here?" the conductor asked.

We all started talking at once. Accusations flew back and forth so fast the poor man told us to be quiet. "You first," he said to Roscoe.

The ugly outlaw drew himself up tall, but he kept a good grip on Calvin. "I'm Mr. Roscoe Suggs," he said, as if the conductor had no doubt heard of him and had always hoped to have the honor of meeting him. Giving Calvin a shake, he added, "This here man and that there boy are wanted for horse theft in Ouray. I got the poster to prove it."

I took a good look at the paper Roscoe showed the conductor. Sure enough, it described a curly-haired youth and a redheaded boy who'd stolen three horses belonging to Mister Roscoe Suggs, Esquire. There was a reward of fifty dollars for our capture. I was a mite disappointed it wasn't a bigger amount, but Roscoe said he was claiming every cent.

"Me and my boys caught these plug-uglies," he boasted. "We know them from way back, and they are surely the most cussed scalawags ever to take a breath of Colorado air. I'll have you know the horses they stole belong to me. Which is why me and my friends here are a-riding on this here train."

The conductor perused the poster, looking from me to Calvin and back again, taking in Caesar, too. I was sorry we didn't look the dandies anymore. If we hadn't been so shabby, things might have gone better with us, as it's a well-known fact that wealth is respected no matter how it's acquired.

"They match the description all right," said the conductor. The Pinkerton thugs nodded. I doubt they were men of many words. "But I ain't sure I trust their safety in your hands, sir."

Roscoe opened his mouth to bellow a protest, but the conductor hushed him. "We'll tie them up nice and secure in the baggage car, sir. Mr. Whipps and Mr. Chaney will keep an eye on them. They are most particular about the care of wanted men, sir."

Here the Pinkerton thugs nodded again, exchanging sharp-toothed grins as they did so.

"When we get to Tinville," the conductor said, "you can take full responsibility for their miserable lives, Mr. Suggs."

"What time will that be?" asked Roscoe, pulling out his watch.

The conductor made a show of looking at his schedule and checking *his* watch. "In one hour and thirty-seven minutes."

Roscoe grumbled and mumbled and confabbed with his cronies, but it was plain the conductor's mind was made up. It was off to the baggage car for Calvin and me.

"What about the mutt?" Shovel Face gazed at Caesar as if he was just itching to kill him.

Before I had a chance to speak up, Roscoe booted Caesar off the platform. I heard my dog yelp, and then he was gone. Using the cuss words I'd learned from frequenting saloons, I hurled myself at Roscoe, but he stopped me with a punch in the side of the head.

The next thing I knew Mr. Whipps was shoving me through the door and into the passenger car. We must have made quite an entrance. Folks stared at us and murmured to one another and asked questions that went unanswered. I kept my head down to hide my tears. My dog was most likely dead and I was going to jail, possibly to be hanged. It seemed my short career as an outlaw was over and my life as well. If Papa was still in Tinville, he'd disown me for shaming him so.

After Mr. Whipps and Mr. Chaney tied us up, the two men gave their attention to a noisy game of cards. Calvin tried to interest them in dealing him a hand, but they said they didn't want no truck with a cheating rascal.

Calvin turned to me and started making excuses for our predicament, but I didn't feel like talking. Or listening. If one of us had to be thrown off the train, I swear I wished it had been the counterfeit outlaw instead of Caesar.

21

WHEN THE TRAIN STOPPED IN TINVILLE, Roscoe entered the car and gave Calvin a kick in the ribs to rouse him. The poor boy got to his feet, looking much the worse for wear. I hadn't noticed his black eye and cut lip, nor had I realized his suit jacket was ripped up the back. He seemed so pitiful I moved a little closer so's he'd know I wasn't mad anymore. Now that we were surrounded by enemies, I figured we'd better take care of each other the best we could.

Calvin caught my eye and smiled, but his eyes stayed just as sad as Caesar's when he was feeling low.

That's when I remembered what Roscoe had done to my dog. I turned on him, hoping to bite him as Caesar would have, but for a fat man Roscoe was fast on his feet. Grabbing my ear, he twisted it hard.

"Behave yourself, boy," he hissed. "You ain't about to pull none of your fancy tricks, nor Featherbone neither. Nobody's got pity for horse thieves in these parts—no matter how young or pretty they are. Why, folks will come from miles away to watch you two dance on air."

"I hate you," I hollered at Roscoe. "You're nothing but a dog-killing no-count drunken skunk!"

Although that earned me a stinging box on the ears, I felt somewhat the better for saying it.

I saw Mr. Whipps grin when I told Roscoe what I thought of him, but he didn't make a move to stop him from hitting me. It was clear he and Mr. Chaney didn't give a hoot about Calvin and me. They just smoked their smelly cigars and drank their coffee. Didn't even wave, much less say good-bye, when Roscoe and his partners dragged Calvin and me off the train.

By the time our little group reached the jailhouse, half of Tinville must have been following us. Most had no idea who Calvin and I were or what we'd done, but they had plenty of opinions. Some thought we were cold-blooded killers. Others believed we'd robbed a string of banks to the south. A few were convinced we'd derailed a train in the New Mexico Territory. I heard more than one claim I wasn't a boy at all but a midget dedicated to a life of crime.

The sheriff and his deputy met us at the jailhouse

door as if they'd been expecting us. I suppose the conductor had wired ahead to warn them a pair of dangerous outlaws were coming their way. When I finally raised my eyes from the sheriff's dusty boots to his face, I saw a tall redheaded man with a gap between his front teeth just like mine.

My heart fell to the bottom of my empty belly and lay there fluttering like a wounded bird. Sheriff Yates was definitely my father. There was no doubt of it. I didn't dare look at him or Calvin. I just stood there wishing I'd never left Kansas.

The deputy was the first to speak. "Why, this boy's the spitting image of you, Alf, right down to his red hair and the gap between his teeth," he said. "He ain't kin to you, is he?"

I felt Calvin staring at me, but I kept my head down. My stomach churned and my mouth filled with hot spit like it does when you're about to throw up. My worst fear had come true. The man Calvin was aiming to kill was my father.

"Elliot, you know I never had a son," Papa said to his deputy. "But if I had, you can bet your life he wouldn't be a common thief like this filthy little guttersnipe."

Turning his attention to Calvin, he continued. "Calvin Featherbone, I arrest you as a horse thief, a liar, a cheat, and a vagabond. Is there anything you want to say in your defense?"

"Only this." Calvin looked Papa in the eye, just as

bold as you please. "Would you kindly tell me whom I have the honor of addressing?"

Papa mulled the words over as if he were translating them from a foreign tongue. "If it's my name you want," he said at last, "I'm Sheriff Alfred Yates, duly elected by the citizens of this town to keep law and order."

"Then you, sir, are my sworn enemy." Calvin spoke softly but his voice just sung with hatred.

While Calvin and Papa eyeballed each other, I stood staring from one to the other, my heart near torn in two. I'd been with Calvin so long, he truly seemed like my brother. I was used to his silly, high-falutin ways. Knew him almost as well as I knew myself. Yet here was Papa, my true blood kin, but a total stranger who'd abandoned me when I was a little child and left me in the hands of hard-hearted relatives who sorely misused me. Who was I supposed to be loyal to?

"I assume this outburst of animosity is related to something of a personal nature," Papa said to Calvin, showing he knew a few good words himself, "and not simply a hatred of the law in general?"

"That is correct, sir." Calvin drew himself up straight. Except for his dirty clothes and unshaven face, he looked a perfect gentleman. "Does not my name sound familiar to you? I am the son of Calvin Thaddeus Featherbone, Senior. A man you cheated and then most vilely shot and killed. A man whose death I have come here to avenge even as Hamlet avenged his father's death!"

Calvin's voice shook and his face was dead white, but he looked Papa in the eye while he made his fancy speech. If Mr. Whipps hadn't taken Calvin's pistol when he arrested him on the train, I was sure my old sidekick would have shot my father, even if it meant his own death.

"I remember your father well," Papa said. "I'm saddened but not surprised to see you have followed his footsteps into a life of crime."

Ignoring a string of poetic curses from Calvin, Roscoe spoke up. He'd been standing beside the Gentleman Outlaw as patient as a groom waiting to exchange wedding vows. "What about my reward, Mr. Sheriff, sir?" he asked, showing off his best manners. "I done brought in two fugitives from justice. How long do I have to wait for my fifty dollars?"

Papa sighed. "The truth of it is I have to wire the sheriff's office in Ouray. I expect they'll have the money here in a day or two."

"A day or two?" Roscoe snorted in disbelief. "I'm a busy man, I got things to do, places to go. That's a 'tarnal long time to keep me waiting for what's due me."

Papa shrugged as if it were of no importance to him what Mr. Roscoe Suggs did. "I suggest you find some business in Tinville to attend to," he said coldly, "but make certain it's legal. I run a tight town. I don't tolerate troublemakers."

"You'll see me tomorrow," Roscoe said, making it sound like a threat. "My reward money better be here and them two crooks better be waiting to do some fancy dancing on the end of a rope."

After Roscoe left, Calvin started to speak, but Papa silenced him. "You can say your piece later, young man. I haven't yet dealt with your accomplice."

"The boy's as innocent as a newborn baby," Calvin said. "Believe me, he—"

"I'll determine his innocence or guilt," Papa said, eyeing me sternly. "State your full name, son."

Gulping hard, I peered into his steely gray eyes, the very ones Mama had once gazed into. What had she seen in their cold depths? I was tempted to say "Elijah Bates" and go to jail with Calvin. Hanging might be better than telling this haughty fellow I was his daughter.

"What's the trouble, boy?" Papa asked with more than a trace of irritation. "Has the cat made off with your tongue?"

Instead of answering him, I turned to Calvin, who was staring at me in a most perplexed way. "It seems I've lied to you," I said. "I apologize for not telling you sooner, but—"

Calvin interrupted me, scowling something fierce. "I knew it all along! Your last name's Yates, isn't it? You're this infamous coward's son!"

I tried to sidle closer to Calvin to soften the blow, but Papa yanked me away so hard he just about dislocated my arm. "What in tarnation is that thieving, no-good rascal talking about?" he hollered at me.

My hand flew to the locket. "Calvin's right about my last name," I said. "It's Yates, though at the moment I wish it wasn't."

Too shamefaced to look at Calvin, I added, "He's wrong about me being your son, though. I'm your daughter, Eliza."

For a moment there wasn't a sound. It was as if everybody in the room had turned to stone. Papa was the first to speak. Stepping toward me, he took hold of my shoulders in a grip so firm and hard I felt it clear down to my bones.

"What sort of low-down tomfoolery is this, boy?" he asked.

For an answer, I dangled the locket in front of him. "Open it. You'll see Mama's face as well as your own."

Papa stared at the miniature portraits. "Where did you steal this, you imp of perdition?"

By now I was crying. "Mama gave it to me before she died," I sobbed. "She told me you were a good man, she said you'd send for me, she said you'd take care of me, but I grew weary of waiting, Papa. I came all this way to find you, and look at the way you're treating me."

All the while I was blubbering to Papa, I could hear Calvin carrying on. He just couldn't believe I'd fooled him so completely. "You should have told me, Eli," he kept saying. "You've made a damned fool out of me!"

Finally Papa told Calvin to be quiet. And the deputy too, for he was running his mouth as well, going on and on about how he knew it the minute he saw me.

"Tarnation, Elliot," Papa said. "I *know* the child looks like me, but I left a *daughter* in Kansas, not a son. How can I be sure this isn't some elaborate hoax dreamed up by Featherbone?"

"Don't lay the blame on me for that perfidious child!" Calvin said, as hot under the collar as an Independence Day firecracker. "I came here to avenge my father, not to engage in asinine games."

Calvin kept on yelling, but neither Papa nor the deputy paid the slightest attention to him.

"You know what I'd do, Alf?" said Elliot.

"Not having been blessed with mind-reading skills, I have no idea what you'd do, Elliot," Papa snapped.

Elliot reached into his pocket for his tobacco. Stuffing a big wad into his cheek, he said, "I'd take the child to Miss Jenny for a bath, which it could surely use as it's contaminating the air."

Papa nodded and took my arm. Turning to the deputy, he said, "Lock up Featherbone, Elliot. I'll leave it to Miss Jenny to be the judge of who or what this child is."

"No, Papa," I cried. "Don't put Calvin in jail. If it hadn't been for him, I'd never have gotten here."

I tried to run to Calvin, but Elliot swatted me aside as if I were no more than an irksome mosquito. As Papa dragged me away, I heard the cell door clang shut. "Traitor!" Calvin yelled after me.

"Step lively," Papa said, pulling me behind him like I was a stubborn donkey. "I have important business to attend to."

I looked back at the jailhouse, but it was all blurry through my tears. First Caesar, now Calvin—I'd lost everybody I cared about just to find a mean-hearted man who still didn't believe I was his daughter. My one wish had been to find my father. It was a mighty cruel world if I had to pay such a terrible price for getting it.

22

OUTSIDE THE JAILHOUSE, THE CROWD HAD vanished except for a few layabouts sitting here and there on railings or loitering by saloons, spitting tobacco and watching Papa quick-march me past. I suppose they wondered what a child my age had done to deserve such treatment. I must confess I wondered myself.

Despite its big hotels and fancy opera house, Tinville seemed no different from every other mining town Calvin and I had gone through on our long journey from Kansas. A little bigger than some, a little smaller than others, but the same old dogs slept in the shade, the same old chickens pecked in the dust, and the same old saloons and stores and livery stables lined the streets. I swear I'd never felt so glum and dispirited in my whole twelve years. It was all I could do not to throw myself down on the ground and cry.

By the time we reached the depot, I was stumbling along, half-blind with tears. Papa hadn't said one word since we'd left the jailhouse. Nor had he let go of my wrist.

Suddenly something caught my eye. I came to a stop and stared down the railroad tracks. Head hanging low, sniffing here and there like he was trying to catch a scent, a dog was limping slowly toward me— a shaggy brown dog I'd thought never to see again.

"Caesar," I hollered, "Caesar!" Breaking away from Papa, I ran to meet my dog, so happy I couldn't do a thing but hug him tight and slobber all over him. "Praise be, you're not dead after all!"

When I finally straightened up, I caught Papa looking at me. It seemed his eyes had gotten a bit softer, but he didn't smile. "I reckon this miserable fleahound is your dog," he said sort of grufflike.

"Yes, sir, he most certainly is. A better dog you'll never find."

Caesar held out his paw to Papa. I reckon he would have showed off every trick he knew if I'd asked him to, but it was pleasing enough to see my father solemnly shake Caesar's paw.

"That villain Roscoe kicked him off the train," I said. "I thought he was dead for sure."

Papa touched my shoulder for just a second. "Come along, you and the dog both. I want you to meet Miss Jenny."

Caesar and I followed Papa up a steep side street to a tidy little house made of wood and painted blue.

A sign in the window said MISS JENNY HAUSMANN, PHOTOGRAPHER.

Papa knocked on the door, and a lady with a no-nonsense look about her opened it. She had brown hair pulled up in an untidy knot on top of her head, and although she was wiping her hands on an apron, there was nothing of the housewife about her. In the sitting room behind her, I caught a glimpse of a big camera on a tripod.

Miss Jenny's smile turned to puzzlement when she saw me. "Why, Alfred, who's this little fellow?"

"Believe it or not, he claims to be my daughter, Eliza," Papa said in a passably humorous way. "I'm turning the rascal over to you. Whichever he is—boy or girl—the child is in desperate need of a bath. When he's clean, tell me what you think of him—or her, as the case may be."

With that, Papa walked away. He had the stiffest back I ever saw.

I turned to Miss Jenny. "No matter what he thinks, he *is* my pa," I said, "but I wish he wasn't. He's got my friend Calvin locked up in jail and he thinks I'm a liar. Which I'm not."

Miss Jenny took my hand. "Whether he's right or wrong to suspect you, Sheriff Yates is most certainly right about one thing," she said in a good-humored voice. "You're in need of a good scrubbing. Once the dirt's gone, I reckon it will be a sight easier to discern your true identity."

I began to object, but Miss Jenny insisted in such

a nice way I ended up following her to the kitchen. Caesar pitter-pattered behind us, still limping a bit. I wanted to tend to him, but Miss Jenny said she knew a lot about dogs. "I'll get to work on him after I finish with you," she promised.

While the water for my bath heated on the stove, Miss Jenny fixed me a nice meal of eggs mixed with potatoes and onions and green peppers. She made sure I had all the bread I wanted and plenty of milk, and she found some treats for Caesar. By the time the bath water was hot, I was full of good food and feeling a tad better about my future.

Which didn't mean I'd forgotten Calvin, who was lodged in my thoughts like a worrisome splinter. I hoped Papa had fed him and talked nice to him and made a friend of him. Surely he'd pardon the Gentleman Outlaw for his crimes, which I knew consisted of no more than stealing a cheap watch and three broken-down horses—unless you counted cheating at cards and lying and being a vagrant.

As for Calvin's hatred of Papa, I imagined it came from some sort of misunderstanding that I'd soon get to the bottom of. Surely a sheriff wouldn't kill a man like Mr. Featherbone, Senior, in cold blood.

Miss Jenny poured hot water into a tin tub and turned her back while I peeled off my dirty clothes. As soon as I was chin deep and decently hid under soapsuds, she commenced to scrub me.

When it felt like she'd just about flayed the skin

off me, Miss Jenny said, "You're crawling with lice, Eliza, and your hair is full of nits."

The way she said my name told me she'd seen enough of me to know for sure I was a girl. Closing my eyes, I let her douse my head with kerosene to exterminate the vermin I'd been harboring for weeks.

"Well," she said, yanking a comb through my hair one last time, "I believe that takes care of the little critters. Lord knows, lice are nothing to be ashamed of. Seems like you can't ride the train these days without catching them."

After I dried off, I followed Miss Jenny into her bedroom. She went through her wardrobe, searching for a dress that might fit me, and came up with a calico she'd shrunk in the wash by accident. It was nicer than anything I'd ever owned, but it felt stiff and tight and I couldn't fasten it without help. What fool thought of putting buttons on the backs of girls' clothes anyway?

When she finished gussying me up, she stood me in front of the mirror. "There," she said, smiling at my reflection. "You look a sight better, Eliza."

I pulled a face. Even though my hair was short, I was most definitely a girl again. In fact, it seemed to me I was more of a girl than I'd been before, if you know what I mean. Elijah was gone—and so were my adventures, sorry as they sometimes were.

Next I'd be washing dishes and sweeping floors

and polishing the furniture. Lord, I might even have to take up embroidery. Begging in saloons and sleeping in caves seemed preferable to spending the rest of my life in petticoats and ruffles.

"Don't worry," Miss Jenny said, thinking to comfort me but guessing at the wrong cause. "When your hair grows back, you'll be the prettiest little gal this side of the Mississippi."

I flung myself on the bed. "Don't want to be pretty," I muttered. "Don't want to be a girl, either."

Miss Jenny sighed and sat down beside me. I expect she thought something was wrong with me. No doubt there was. What kind of girl doesn't want to be a girl? I hid my face, sure Miss Jenny was about to give me a tongue lashing that would no doubt include words from the Bible and threats of hellfire.

She took a deep breath, but before she had a chance to speak her mind, someone commenced knocking on the back door. The noise set Caesar to barking.

While I hushed my dog, Miss Jenny welcomed Papa into her little kitchen. Waving one hand at me, she said, "Whether or not she's your daughter I can't say, but the child's a girl beyond all doubt."

Papa studied me hard. Suddenly his eyes filled with tears. "Eliza's mine all right," he said. "Now she's dressed proper I see her mother in every feature except her hair. She got that from me, right down to the last curl."

He took me in his arms, as shy as a stranger, and gave me a hug and kiss. "I'm sorry I doubted you, Eliza," he whispered.

According to Miss Jenny, it was a right touching scene. She said later if she'd seen it on stage, she'd have wept for a week. Even the hardest-hearted man would have broken down and sobbed, she claimed. It was that moving to see a father and daughter reunited at last.

When Papa could speak, he explained why— aside from my appearance—he'd doubted me. "I just mailed your allowance to Mabel and Homer. Why didn't they tell me you were coming?"

I stared at Papa, amazed. "You've been sending me money?"

It was Papa's turn to stare. "Of course I have. What sort of man do you take me for? I've been wiring ten dollars every month since I got word of your mother's death."

"That's the first I ever heard about any money," I said, astonished by the news. "Aunt Mabel and Uncle Homer told me you'd disappeared and were most likely dead or in jail."

"I don't understand," said Papa, his face awash with confusion. "Didn't they give you my letters?"

I shook my head.

"But there was a message from you in every letter they sent me."

"Well, it surely wasn't me that wrote it."

Papa was flummoxed. He sputtered and hemmed and hawed and got red in the face. "I trusted Homer and Mabel to take care of you. They said you were like a daughter to them."

"More like a slave," I muttered, remembering beatings and whippings and going without dinner and being locked in the fruit cellar to repent my sins. There was no sense telling Papa about all the grief I'd endured from those kindly souls, so I contented myself with saying, "They lied to us both, Papa. And cheated us too. Just take a look at this."

I reached into my dress pocket and pulled out the newspaper clipping I'd been saving since I left Miss Pearl's house in Kansas. "Aunt Mabel and Uncle Homer think I'm dead—yet they're still taking your money!"

Papa read the story of my murder slowly and carefully. When he finished, he gazed at me sadly. "I made a terrible mistake, Eliza. I hope you'll forgive me for trusting your well-being to those heartless scoundrels."

Although I don't think of myself as a calculating individual out to take advantage of other folks' guilt, I must admit Papa's words gave me an idea. Edging closer to him, I peered into his eyes, hoping shamelessly to melt his heart like Millicent would have. "Of course I forgive you, Papa, but . . ." Here I paused to toy with the gold star pinned to his coat.

"But what?" Papa asked in a tender way.

"Well," I said, "I hope you'll remember all Calvin did to get me here safely. It seems to me he deserves a reward, but instead, he's locked up in jail."

Papa sighed. "Life's a mixture, Eliza. It was good Calvin brought you here, but the way he did it was bad. Stealing horses is a crime. You can't ignore the law. If everyone did as he pleased, what would happen to civilization?"

Sometimes I thought we'd be better off without so much civilization, but I knew better than to say that to Papa. "Well," I said, "how about shooting unarmed men in the back? Do you call that civilized?"

Papa looked puzzled. "What has shooting a man in the back got to do with Calvin's being in jail?"

"It's why Calvin hates you, Papa." I stared him straight in the eye, daring him to lie. "He claims that's what you did to his father. Killed him in cold blood."

"Calvin told you that?" Papa spoke as if he could scarcely believe his ears. "The truth is Featherbone was a desperado, Eliza—a cheat, a thief, and a killer. Why, he was wanted in every town in the West. It was he who started the shooting, not me. By the time I got to the Emerald Saloon, he'd already killed two gamblers and wounded three others—all because they'd caught him cheating and had the temerity to say so."

I stared at Papa, my head whirling with confusion. "Calvin says *you* cheated *him* and then shot him down in the street. Left him to die in the dirt. It's all in a letter he showed me. I read it myself, Papa."

"The Lord only knows who wrote him such a passel of lies," Papa said. "I shot Featherbone in self-defense. Elliot was there, he can testify to it."

"Your father's telling the truth," Miss Jenny said. "Featherbone's death was written up in the paper. Why, I even photographed his body. The bullet hit him in the chest, not in the back."

"You'd better tell Calvin that," I said. "Knowing him, it will take a sight of fancy talk to persuade him it's true."

"Most likely it will," Papa said, "but I'm right good at speechifying when I put my mind to it."

I noticed he winked at Miss Jenny when he said this, and she blushed a pretty shade of pink.

"Calvin's not a bad man, Papa, just a mite confused about things." I tried the girly trick of batting my eyelashes. It always worked for Millicent. Maybe it would for me, too. "If you were to let Calvin out of jail, I bet he'd never trouble you again."

"Well, now, Eliza, I'm afraid I can't do that. I've notified the sheriff in Ouray already. He's sending a man to fetch Calvin. He should arrive on the train tomorrow evening."

I gasped. "Is he coming for me too?"

Papa shook his head and smiled. "Why, how can

he, Eliza? Elijah Bates has mysteriously vanished from the face of the earth. Nobody knows where that boy went."

Glad as I was to know I was safe, I couldn't let the subject drop. I tried to persuade Papa to free Calvin, but even though I argued till I was near speechless, Papa was just as determined to keep the Gentleman Outlaw in jail as I was determined to get him out.

Finally Papa said if I mentioned Calvin's name one more time, he'd string him up himself. That shut my mouth. But it didn't stop me from thinking. There had to be some way to get Calvin out of jail.

23

THE NEXT MORNING, MISS JENNY TIED A BON-
net under my chin to hide my short hair and
took me to a dressmaker. She ordered me a whole
set of ruffled girls' clothes that weighed me down
with so much gingham and calico I could hardly
walk, let alone run.

If that wasn't bad enough, Papa tied up Caesar,
something my old pal hadn't experienced since
we'd run off from Uncle Homer's place. Papa said
it was for his own good. Caesar was weak from the
hardships he'd suffered. If he wandered away, he
might meet up with a pack of stray dogs and fare
poorly.

Maybe Papa was right, but it just about broke my
heart to see poor Caesar lying in the hot sun, looking so pitiful. He couldn't understand what he'd
done to be punished so.

Worst of all, Calvin stayed locked up. Papa wouldn't

even let me visit him. The jailhouse was no place for a girl, he said.

It seemed Calvin, Caesar, and I had come all this way only to end up no happier than we'd been in Kansas. It was a mighty disappointing turn of events.

→>·<←

Just as I was getting as sorrowful as sorrowful can be, things improved unexpectedly. Papa had come by for dinner, and we were still sitting at the table when a visitor came to the front door—Mr. Roscoe Suggs himself. Before Miss Jenny let him in, I scurried out of sight behind some drapes. But not out of earshot.

"Your deputy told me I'd find you here, Sheriff Yates," Roscoe said as bold as you please. "I came to see about my fifty-dollar reward."

Papa reached into his pocket and took out five gold eagles. "The money came this morning," he said, handing the coins to Roscoe.

Through an opening in the drapes, I watched Roscoe drop the money into *his* pocket. "Thank you, sir," he said, making the words sound more like an insult than an expression of gratitude. "I'm glad to see you still have that plug-ugly in the lockup. The world will be safer for us honest folks when the rascal's hanged, but I can't help wondering where the boy is. Your deputy clammed up tight as a fresh oyster when I asked."

"It appears the boy has a relative in town," Papa said. "Believe me, he's the sort who'll make sure the little rascal behaves himself."

It seemed to me Papa raised his voice while delivering this bit of information. Perhaps he intended it for my ears as well as Roscoe's.

"Well, now, I'm mighty pleased to hear that," said Roscoe. "As the Bible says, spare the rod and spoil the child. Whippings and beatings aplenty—that's the way the good Lord wants us to bring up our progeny."

Flashing his gold tooth at Miss Jenny in what he no doubt fancied was a charming way, Roscoe bade Papa good-bye and swaggered off toward Harrison Avenue and the saloons that lined it.

Before Papa or Miss Jenny noticed me, I grabbed my bonnet and scampered out the back door. It didn't take long to catch up with Roscoe. I skipped past him, acting as girly-girly as I could, and pretended to trip over his foot. Even though I fell on purpose, I knocked the wind right out of myself.

Just as I'd hoped, Roscoe leaned down and helped me up. "Why, bless your little heart, darling, did I hurt you?"

He wouldn't have spoken so kindly if two ladies hadn't been standing a few feet away, twirling their parasols and watching him closely. It was clear they were prepared to attack at the first sign of rudeness or indifference on his part. Make no mistake, they seemed to say, men who trip little girls are not looked upon favorably in Tinville.

Playing the part of a helpless creature, I pressed my hand to my heart. "I feel faint, sir," I whispered. "Could you please help me home?"

With those ladies watching, there was nothing for Roscoe to do but take my arm. "I'm sure I never meant to trip you," he murmured, trying to hide his true villainy.

"I believe you, sir," I said, smiling as sweetly as the sweetest of girls.

He peered at me. "What's your name, honey? You look strangely familiar."

"Eliza Yates," I said. "Perhaps you know my papa, Sheriff Alfred Yates? Folks say I resemble him most remarkably."

"The sheriff's little daughter," Roscoe said. "My, my, it's a pleasure to meet you, darling. I paid your papa a visit just a few minutes ago."

He stopped to give my hand a little squeeze. "I hope you won't tell your Papa I tripped you, Miss Eliza. I sure wouldn't want him thinking ill of me."

"Oh no, sir," I assured him, smiling so hard my whole face ached with the terrible effort. "It's plain to see you're a perfect gentleman, not at all the sort to cause harm to an innocent creature—child or animal."

Roscoe flashed that gold tooth again, and we walked on. Still feigning weakness, I leaned against his side, forcing him to support me. Before we reached Miss Jenny's front gate, I managed to slip my fingers into Roscoe's pocket. Remembering everything I'd learned from watching Calvin, I pulled out the five eagles he'd wrapped in his handkerchief. Slowly and carefully, I transferred them to my pocket. The Gentleman Outlaw would have been proud to see how deftly I did it. The coins didn't even clink.

Just as Roscoe opened the gate, Papa came out the front door. "Eliza," he cried, "what's the trouble? Are you hurt?"

"I tripped and fell, Papa," I murmured. "This kind gentleman brought me home."

Papa looked perplexed, but before he could ask me any questions, I slipped through the gate and darted up the porch steps. Miss Jenny opened the door, and I ran inside, followed by Papa.

"What happened, Eliza?" Miss Jenny asked, sounding every bit as puzzled as Papa. "Did you hurt yourself? Do you feel ill?"

Without answering, I peeked out the window. Roscoe was meandering along, just as pleased with himself as he could be. Now that I'd gotten what I wanted from my enemy, I turned to Papa.

"That man is an outlaw," I announced. "It's him who should be in jail, not Calvin. If you let him leave town free as a bird, he'll have made a monkey of you and the law, Papa."

Papa studied me a minute. "Are you telling the truth, Eliza? Or just seeking revenge?"

I felt my face heat up with anger. Papa still doubted me. Speaking fast, I told him of my first encounter with Roscoe and everything that had happened since. "He tried to kill Calvin more than once," I finished up, "and me too. Lord, Papa, a man who'd kick a poor dog off a moving train has got to be a low-down, worthless good-for-nothing!"

"Now that I think about it, Eliza, Mr. Suggs did look familiar," Papa said, buckling on his holster as he spoke. "I believe I've seen him in Tinville before. Perhaps I'll invite him to drop by the jailhouse for a friendly little chat."

→>•◄←

When Papa showed up for supper that night, he thanked me for telling him about Roscoe. "It seems Mr. Suggs is wanted in every state and territory west of the Mississippi," he said. "We'll be collecting a nice reward for his capture, Eliza. To think I almost let that skunk walk out of Tinville scot-free!"

"Papa, you didn't put Roscoe in the same cell as Calvin, did you?" If he had, there was no telling what Roscoe might do to my poor friend.

"Of course not," Papa said, speaking as if I'd

insulted him. "Tinville's a prosperous city. One cell couldn't hold all our criminals." He laughed. "Why, Tinville is so full of crooks poor old Roscoe had his pocket picked in broad daylight. Lost every cent of his reward money before he could gamble it away at the faro table."

Miss Jenny chuckled and said it served him right. I joined in the hilarity, hoping nobody suspected I had anything to do with Roscoe's misfortune.

To change the subject, I asked Papa if he'd told Calvin the truth about his father.

"Yes, I did, but I had the devil of a time convincing him. That young man threw so many long words my way he almost knocked me out with the weight of them."

Papa paused to light his pipe before going on. "If it hadn't been for Elliot, I don't believe Calvin would have accepted my version of his daddy's death, but fortunately Elliot saves wanted posters. He found three featuring Calvin Thaddeus Featherbone, Senior, as well as a newspaper account written the day after the shooting, laying out the facts as I told them."

"Poor boy," Miss Jenny said. "It must have been a terrible disappointment to learn his father was a no-good scoundrel."

"He was mighty glum," Papa admitted, "but he perked up a sight when he saw we'd arrested Roscoe. I left the two of them hurling insults back and forth.

Calvin was definitely getting the better of Roscoe, who tends to be a bit slow-witted to say the least."

It looked like Papa was finished talking, but there was one more thing I was curious about. "Did Calvin show you the letter his mother got?" I asked.

Papa nodded. "Elliot and I figured it was written by one of Mr. Featherbone's lady friends. Probably Miss Flora. She kicked up a terrible ruckus after the shooting. Went from saloon to saloon, seeking vengeance. When nobody offered to shoot me, I reckon she wrote to Mrs. Featherbone, hoping Calvin Junior would ride into town on a white horse and do the job."

When Papa paused again to fidget with his pipe, Miss Jenny said, "At least Flora had the decency not to sign her name to that letter. No sense hurting a widow's feelings."

"Where's Miss Flora now?" I asked Papa.

"Oh, she left Tinville a month or two ago. I reckon she grew weary of waiting for your friend to appear."

Miss Jenny excused herself to fix a pot of tea. When she came back, she and Papa began talking of the new minister who was preaching against saloons, gambling houses, and dance halls. Seemed like a number of townspeople agreed with his views. Wouldn't be long before they cleaned up Harrison Avenue, Papa said. Times were changing. Civilization was taking over everywhere.

Left to my own thoughts, I contemplated Papa's

jacket hanging over the back of a chair. In its pocket were the keys to the jail. If I could get my hands on them, I could free Calvin.

24

AFTER SUPPER, MISS JENNY SUGGESTED A
game of dominos. I said I was too tired to play,
but I hung around watching for a few minutes. When
I was sure Papa and Miss Jenny were paying more
attention to the dominos than to me, I slipped my
hand into the pocket of Papa's jacket and pulled
out his keys without his noticing a thing. It scared me
to discover how easy thievery is. I hoped I wasn't
heading for a life of crime after all, but I supposed I
could always reform after Calvin was safely out of jail.

I yawned real wide and said I was going to bed.
Papa gave me a kiss and wished me sweet dreams,
which made me feel powerful bad. But not bad
enough to stop myself from climbing out the bedroom window, which wasn't easy in a dress, and
untying Caesar's rope. I'd have given anything for
my boy clothes, but Miss Jenny had burned them to
get rid of the vermin breeding in every seam.

Slowed by skirts and petticoats, I ran down the street with Caesar at my heels. Somewhere on Harrison Avenue, I bumped right into a tall, skinny man. He'd just stepped out of a saloon doorway, and he spun around to face me. I must have startled him, for he was pointing a gun right at me.

"Lord, don't shoot," I cried.

The man smiled and dropped his gun into his holster. "I'm not in the habit of killing ladies, big or small," said he.

The moon was shining full on his face, and I recognized the mysterious gentleman who'd given me those gold eagles way back in Pueblo. He looked a sight the worse for wear. Thinner, paler. At death's door, Aunt Mabel would have said.

"You don't remember me, sir," I said, "but you did me a favor once."

"Why, I'm mighty pleased to hear it," he said. "These days, I rarely meet a person who doesn't hold a grudge against me for one thing or another."

"I was traveling with a fellow by the name of Calvin Featherbone. He's in jail now," I went rushing on as if I were telling my life history, but the man seemed right kindly and in no hurry to leave. "My papa put him there," I said. "Maybe you know him. He's Alfred Yates, the sheriff."

The man smiled. "Yes, indeed, I know your father well." He looked at me curiously. "But I must admit I don't recall meeting a young girl on my travels."

"It was a while back, in Pueblo," I said, "but I wasn't a girl then. I was a boy."

"Indeed?" The gentleman scrutinized my face and laughed till he brought on a coughing fit. When he recovered, he said, "I've encountered many a peculiarity since I left Georgia, but this may be the oddest tale yet. Tell me, dear, how did you accomplish this amazing transformation?"

"Just by wearing boys' clothes and giving myself a boy's name," I said. "It's amazing how easy it was to fool everybody, even Calvin."

The man smiled as if he wanted to laugh but was afraid of bringing on another coughing fit. "Is Calvin by any chance the young rogue who was so adept at three-card monte and so inept at the faro table?"

"Yes, sir, that's him," I said, "but he improved considerably at gambling."

"Yet he's in jail."

"For horse theft," I admitted. "It seems he wasn't very good at that."

The man shook his head. "Too bad," he mused. "I've been in jail myself a few times. It's not a pleasant experience."

Before I could say more, a man stepped out of the saloon. "Come back inside, Doc," he said with the utmost courtesy. "We're waiting on you to deal."

I stared at the man, almost but not quite speechless. "Are you Doc Holliday?"

He bowed like a true gentleman. "I am indeed, my dear."

"Doc!" someone hollered from the saloon.

"Excuse me," Doc said to me, "but the four queens require my company."

I stood there, taking him in, memorizing every detail from his drooping mustache to his ruffled shirt and diamond rings. Doc Holliday. The most famous desperado of all. The one nobody could outdraw or outplay or outtalk. I was looking right at him, standing only a few inches away, breathing the same air he breathed.

Doc touched my shoulder as if he was waking me from a dream. "I suggest you go home, my little daisy, before mischief claims you."

"Wait," I whispered. "I have to ask you something."

Doc turned back. "What is it, sweetheart?"

"Do you remember Calvin's father, a dealer named Calvin Thaddeus Featherbone, Senior?"

Doc thought a moment. The lines around his mouth deepened. "So that's why the boy looked familiar," he muttered almost as if he were speaking to himself, not me. "I do recall the man, Eliza, and I must say I'm sorry to hear he's your friend's father. A worse miscreant I never encountered. A despicable cheat, a liar, and a coward. Had the temper of a rattlesnake. Why, he'd shoot a man just as soon as look at him."

Turning away to cough into a lacy handkerchief,

Holliday went on as soon as he could speak. "Featherbone Senior is one of the few men I can safely accuse of being worse than myself. Tell Calvin to go back home before he follows in his father's cheating footsteps."

"He's got to get out of jail first," I said.

Doc smiled. "I'm sure a girl with your wits will find a way to accomplish his escape."

So saying, he bade me good night and vanished into the smoky saloon.

I stood there awhile listening to the honky-tonk piano music and the sound of men's laughter. Caesar pawed my leg and barked. I suppose he wanted to follow Doc inside and relive his glory days, performing tricks and such. If it hadn't been for poor Calvin, that's just what I would have done. Lord, what a memory that would be—seeing Doc Holliday at the faro table. But I couldn't keep Calvin waiting.

Turning away reluctantly, I crept down the alley behind the jailhouse and stopped under a barred window. Whipping out my harmonica, I commenced to play "O, Susanna!" Caesar raised up on his hind legs and sang along just as if we were doing a show.

In no time, Calvin was peering out at me. "Stop that racket, little girl. You'll wake the dead."

It peeved me he didn't recognize me. Whipping off my bonnet, I scowled at him. "If I can't get you out of here, you're going to be in the graveyard sleeping with the dead yourself. No matter how much racket I make, I won't be able to wake you then."

Calvin took a good look at me and chuckled. "If you aren't a sight in that dress. No wonder I never suspected. Clothes might make the gentleman but they certainly don't make the lady."

Though I hate to admit it, I'd been secretly hoping to impress Calvin. His teasing words hurt me more than I'd thought possible. "Don't you go making fun of me," I said, "or I'll leave you here to dance on the end of a rope."

"Oh, Eli." Calvin's voice dropped down way below serious, more dejected than I'd ever heard it. "Much as I appreciate your concern, I don't think there's anything you can do to prevent me from swinging."

"Don't say that." I rose up on tiptoe, grabbed the bars on his window, and hoisted myself high enough to look him in the eye. "I've got the key. I stole it out of Papa's pocket."

I dug my toes into the wall to keep from slipping back to the ground and showed Calvin the key ring, but the sight of it didn't cheer him one iota.

"How do you plan to get past the deputy, Eli?"

I slid down the wall and landed hard on my backside. I hadn't counted on the deputy being at the jailhouse. A vague recollection of a story I'd heard about Doc Holliday floated through my head. He'd been in jail, all set to be hanged, but his lady friend Big Nose Kate rescued him by setting a fire behind a fancy hotel. Everybody ran to put it out, Kate shot the guard, sprung Doc, and the two of them lit out for Dodge City.

The trouble was I had neither matches nor gun, and even if I had, I doubted I was up to setting a fire or shooting Elliot who seemed to be a nice man.

A better idea came to mind. "Don't you worry, Calvin. I'll get you out of there."

Leaving him staring after me, I ran down the alley and dashed into the jailhouse. Elliot was sitting behind the desk, feet propped up, reading the latest issue of *Police Gazette*. He dropped the magazine when he saw me. "Who the dickens are you and what do you want?"

"It's me, Eliza Yates," I cried. "Sheriff Yates's daughter. Don't you remember?"

Elliot stared at me. "Why, pardon me, Miss Eliza. I didn't recognize you," he apologized. "Miss Jenny sure has done wonders with your appearance."

"Thank you," I said, remembering the manners Calvin had taken such pains to teach me. "Papa sent me to tell you he needs help at the Diamond Saloon. Doc Holliday's on the rampage."

"Oh, Lord," Elliot whispered. "What's Doc doing here? Last I heard he was in Glenwood Springs, dying of consumption." Jumping to his feet, he ran out the door and vanished into the dark.

Faster than you can say "Jack Robinson's barn," I unlocked the jail door and out came Calvin.

"What the devil's going on?" bellowed a familiar voice from the adjoining cell. Caesar almost tore down the bars trying to get at Roscoe, but I grabbed him and held tight.

While Calvin smoothed his hair and preened, Roscoe raised a ruckus, making enough noise to wake snakes.

"You thieving little cuss," he hollered at me. "It was you in that dress! First you stole my reward money and then you turned me in to the sheriff! I should've killed you when I had the chance, you and Featherbone both!"

It appeared Calvin was about to start an argument, so I grabbed his arm. "Come on, Calvin, you haven't got time for any shenanigans!"

With that, the two of us headed for the hills, running like the north wind, with Caesar following close behind. How Papa would feel didn't bear considering. Right now I just wanted to get Calvin out of Tinville as fast as I could. I'd worry about Papa later.

25

ONCE WE'D PUT A FEW BLOCKS BETWEEN US and the jailhouse, Calvin came to a halt. "There's something I have to see before I leave Tinville," he said.

Argue as I might, there was no changing Calvin's mind. Sticking to the shadows, he led me to a graveyard on the outskirts of town. "Your papa told me where it was," he explained as I followed him through the gate.

In the moonlight, the burial ground was a scary place, bare and dusty. A few scrawny trees cast shadows over the hillside. There were lots of graves, mostly marked by crooked wooden slabs and surrounded with spindly little fences, making them resemble cribs for sleeping children. Clumps of sagebrush grew here and there, and the wind sighed sadly through them.

Calvin stared at the desolate sight. "In Maryland,

cemeteries are as green as parks," he said slowly. "Winding boulevards, groves of trees, ponds, flowers, marble headstones, cenotaphs, angels, rows of mausoleums as fine as mansions."

I shivered and said nothing. Caesar was roaming around sniffing the ground as if he knew bones were buried there. Keeping an eye on my dog, I took care not to step on anybody's grave. Aunt Mabel taught me you'd have bad luck all your life if you disturbed the dead.

"Are we looking for your papa?" I whispered, afraid to speak normally in such a place.

Calvin nodded. "Your father told me his friend Miss Flora raised the money to bury him here. He said the townspeople didn't want a criminal interred with the righteous, so his grave is at the top of the hill beside the fence, as far as possible from everyone else's."

When we finally found Featherbone Senior's burial place, Calvin took off his hat and stared solemnly at the wooden marker. It leaned forward, worn and weathered as if it had been there a hundred years or more. From what we made out, it said, HERE LIES CALVIN FEATHERBONE, SENIOR. 1839–1887. HE HAS BEEN DEALT HIS FINAL HAND.

The ground covering Mr. Featherbone was dry and rocky, and his little picket fence was falling down on one side. It was a mighty sad spot for a man to spend eternity, I thought.

Calvin fetched up a sigh as mournful as the wind. "It seems I've come all this way merely to discover my father was a worse cheat than I and no doubt deserved to be shot," he said with some bitterness. "It's obvious neither my name nor his will be preserved in the annals of the Wild West. Or anywhere else, for that matter."

I touched his sleeve, as worried by his sorrow as if it were mine. "What are you fixing to do now, Calvin?"

"From what I've seen of the outlaw life, I fear it's vastly overrated," he said glumly.

Since I'd reached the same conclusion myself, I was glad to hear Calvin had come to his senses at last.

"Before I left home," Calvin went on, "I was planning to enter Johns Hopkins University in Baltimore—at Grandfather's expense. If he can find it in his heart to forgive my foolish and ungrateful behavior, I believe I'll continue my education."

He paused and studied his father's grave for a moment. "I certainly don't intend to end my days in a place like this."

"Me either," I agreed.

We stared at each other. The wind breathed and sighed around us, and the moon slid behind a cloud like it was too shy to show its face. For a moment, I glimpsed something I'd never seen in Calvin's eyes. A tenderness, I swear that's what it was, but I could have been mistaken. Suddenly embarrassed, I kicked at a tumbleweed rolling past.

Calvin broke the silence. "I'd best be going, Eli."

I grabbed hold of his arm. "Wait," I said. Reaching into my pocket, I pulled out the coins I'd taken from Roscoe and put them in his hand.

Calvin stared at the gold eagles. "Fifty dollars," he whispered. "Where did you get this, Eli? Surely you didn't purloin it from your father?"

"There you go again with those highfalutin words. I didn't purloin it from anybody—whatever that means. I stole it right out of Roscoe's pocket. It's the reward money he got for turning you in. It's only right you should have it."

Calvin laughed and dropped the coins into his pocket. Then he looked at me seriously. "I don't know why I never noticed how pretty you are, Eli— I mean, Eliza."

I blushed in the most girlish way imaginable. "Do you really think I'm pretty?"

"Have you ever known me to prevaricate?"

I hauled off to punch him, but Calvin was too fast for me. Before I guessed what he was up to, he'd given me a peck on the cheek.

"That's so you'll remember me," he said, stepping away. "No girl ever forgets the man who gives her her first kiss."

Without letting me say another word, Calvin hopped the cemetery fence and strode off toward the mountains. Caesar started to follow him but turned back when I whistled. Like my dog, I was tempted to run after Calvin and beg him to take me with him, but I stayed where I was, gripping the iron railing and thinking of Papa. Now that I'd finally found him, I couldn't very well run off and leave him.

At a bend in the trail, Calvin paused to wave. "I'll see you again, Eliza," he called. "Wait and see."

So saying, Calvin vanished into the night, and Caesar and I were alone in the cemetery with nothing but a chilly wind whispering sad songs in our ears.

26

WHEN I GOT TO MISS JENNY'S HOUSE, THE moon was low in the sky. I'd taken my time walking back from the cemetery, for I knew I was about to get the worst whipping of my life. Spilling milk and jam was nothing compared to helping an outlaw escape from jail. The only thing in my favor was I hadn't started a fire or killed anybody.

Coming up the walk, I saw Papa sitting on the front porch, but the light was too dim to read the look on his face.

I climbed the steps as slowly as I dared. If Papa had been Uncle Homer, he'd have been on his feet, hollering my name and cracking the air with his belt. But Papa stayed seated and spoke soft, putting me in mind of deadly copperheads that strike without warning.

Fixing me with a stern eye, Papa said, "Well, Eliza, what am I going to tell the deputy from Ouray when he comes to collect his prisoner tomorrow evening?"

I swallowed hard and faced Papa. My lying days were over. "Calvin's my friend," I said. "I had to save him from hanging."

"What the devil for?" Papa's voice rose and his face turned redder than his hair. It appeared he was working himself up into a temper after all. "The boy's bound and determined to follow in his father's footsteps—cheating folks at cards, lying and stealing, corrupting innocent children!"

"Calvin didn't corrupt me! I've been bad all my life. Just ask Aunt Mabel. She'll say it was you I got it from."

I was hollering so loud Miss Jenny came to the door and peered out at Papa and me. I don't know what we'd have said or done next if she hadn't burst out laughing. "Lord, the two of you are a fine pair," she said. "Just look at your fiery faces. If I had any doubts about Eliza being your daughter, Alfred, they're gone now."

Papa stared at Miss Jenny. "What in tarnation is so blamed funny? Eliza let that scoundrel go! And more's the pity, she's not even sorry!"

"Now, Alfred," Miss Jenny said, still grinning, "you know full well prisoners escape from that jail with amazing regularity. No one need know Eliza had a thing to do with Calvin's disappearance."

Papa ignored Miss Jenny. "Your little prank almost got my deputy killed, Eliza."

"What do you mean?"

"The poor man went running into the Diamond Saloon, gun drawn, ready to shoot. Holliday was on his feet in a second, pointing his revolver straight at Elliot's heart." Papa paused, to let me think about that, I guess.

"Luckily Elliot had the good sense to drop his gun fast and raise his hands," Papa went on. "Seeing nothing but a game of faro, he apologized. Doc bought him a whiskey and that was that."

Papa eyed me steadily. "It could have gone differently, Eliza. Holliday has shot men for a sight less than what Elliot did."

I felt so heavy with remorse I feared I might sink right through the porch floor. "I never dreamed anything of the sort would happen, Papa."

He just looked at me. Miss Jenny had stopped smiling. She didn't have anything to say either. Papa's chair squeaked as he shifted his weight. It was the only sound except for the soft din coming from the saloons down the hill on Harrison Avenue.

Finally Miss Jenny broke the silence. "What's done is done," she said softly. "Why don't we go inside? I believe it's almost time for breakfast."

By the time we finished eating, Papa had agreed to cover up my part in Calvin's escape if I promised to go down to the jailhouse and apologize to Elliot for jeopardizing his life. I was glad to say I would.

"Now that our unpleasant business is out of the way," Papa said, "we have other matters to discuss, Eliza."

Taking Miss Jenny's hand, he went on, "If Jenny ever sets the date, I plan to marry her someday."

He paused to give me time to digest the news, but any fool could have seen there was something of a romantical nature cooking between the two of them. The only thing that surprised me was Miss Jenny's failure to name the day. According to Aunt Mabel, most women leaped at the chance to snare a husband.

"Till Jenny becomes my wife," Papa went on, "we're hoping you won't mind living here. Elliot and I share a room at Widow McGraw's boarding-house, a respectable place but not fit for a girl."

I assured Papa I'd be happy to stay with Miss Jenny, having had my fill of hotels and boarding-houses. My answer pleased them both. When Papa left for work, he was whistling despite the fact he'd gotten no sleep, thanks to me.

→>•<←

After we cleared the table, I helped Miss Jenny wash the dishes, a chore I hadn't done for a long, long time. I hated it just as much as I remembered.

When we were finishing up, Miss Jenny asked me where Calvin had gone.

"He's heading back to Baltimore," I told her, feeling a heaviness in my chest I'd never experienced before. "He plans to finish his schooling there."

"That sounds like a fine idea," Miss Jenny said. "According to your daddy, Calvin's a smart young man, though lacking a sense of direction in life. A good education may set him on the right course."

"I reckon," I said, hoping I wasn't developing a weak heart.

"What about you, Eliza?" Miss Jenny asked. "Have you thought about what you want to do?"

"Me?" Surprised by the question, I scowled at the greasy pan I was drying. "What choice do I have? I'll either get married or, more likely, live out my days as an old maid."

"Surely you don't believe that, Eliza."

I stared at Miss Jenny, flummoxed. She'd been a girl herself and not that long ago. Had she already forgotten how it was?

"Miss Jenny," I said, speaking slowly so she'd be sure to understand, "you know full well girls aren't supposed to do anything but sit and sew and act ladylike in hope of catching a husband."

"For heaven's sake," Miss Jenny said, sounding a bit riled. "I'm not married, but I don't think of myself as an old maid."

So saying, she led me into the room where she kept her camera and showed me the pictures she'd taken. Some were portraits and some were landscapes. Every one of them showed you something you might not have noticed otherwise. The way sun shines on a brick wall, for instance, or the shape of a shadow on the ground. A plume of smoke from a steam locomotive or a look in a woman's eyes that gives away her secrets.

"This is my work," Miss Jenny said, sounding as fierce as Calvin when he used to talk about vengeance and such. "It's what I do. Married or single, I'll always be a photographer, never an old maid."

I studied Miss Jenny's pictures, taken by the way they caught a moment of a person's life and preserved it forever. Long after the folks who posed for Miss Jenny were dead and gone, even if nobody remembered who they were, their faces would be here, proving they'd lived on earth a while—been happy or sad, pretty or plain, fat or thin. I thought of the weeks I'd spent with Calvin, of the people and places I'd seen, and wished I'd had a camera to save it all from slipping out of my head.

"Is it hard to take pictures, Miss Jenny?"

She thought a moment, showing she wasn't the sort who gives easy answers to keep a person from asking more questions. "Anyone can learn the mechanics of photography," she said. "What's hard is taking a *good* picture. For that, you need a sharp eye, a great deal of patience, and years of practice."

Miss Jenny paused and looked at me closely. "If you're interested," she said, "I could use some help with things like changing portrait backdrops, loading the flash pan, developing the plates, and so on."

I jumped at the offer, partly because I was hoping to get out of doing chores of the domestic kind but also because it sounded a heap more interesting than learning to embroider and crochet and sew a fine seam, which was what most girls did in their spare time.

Miss Jenny smiled and put her arm around me. I leaned against her for a moment, enjoying the comfort of a motherly embrace which I had sorely missed.

After Miss Jenny left the room I lingered at the window, thinking of Calvin. Someday he'd come walking up the hill to Miss Jenny's little house. I knew he would. Why, I could see him just as clear as if he was already there. When he knocked at the door, I'd invite him in. After he got used to the shock of seeing me all grown up, I'd pose him for a portrait. The "Reformed Outlaw," I'd call it.

Then, a hundred or more years from now, a person might come across the photograph. A girl maybe, no older than me. She'd stare at Calvin's face and wonder who that handsome gentleman was. She might even make up her own story about him. But I doubt it would be any better than mine—which happens to be the truth.